A Few Seconds in Between

Randy A. Green

Dedication

To my Grandson Everett, may you rise up to meet the challenges you will face with grace, dignity and determination. You will forever be loved unconditionally.

Prologue

Writing a book is easier than I expected, it's getting lots of people to read it that is the hard part. This story pushed me far beyond my literary comfort zone for many reasons. It mixes drama with imagination, and spirituality with Sci-fi. It is your choice as to how you interpret it. Either way, I do hope you enjoy it for I have managed to keep it imprisoned within the confines of my laptop for a few years and without the help of some very special friends, especially my sister Rhonda, it would have never been paroled. I received amazing feedback from friends and family but more importantly I received much needed encouragement from all of them in gigantic proportions. I am so blessed to have friends that aren't afraid to tell me when I am wrong and family that put up with me in spite of it. Indulge me if you can, enjoy the book and if for a fleeting moment you forget about your worries and get lost in this story, then I have accomplished what I intended because I think we all spend far too much time agonizing over our past instead of enthusiastically attacking our future.

Chapter 1

"COME ON, LETS GO THIS WAY." Gail was an adventuresome geologist who had a passion for cave mapping and exploration. Being an adrenaline junkie and risk taker, it consumed her. Hollis was more pragmatic, but also shared Gail's passion for geology but not the passion for cave dwelling. She tended to like open air and the geological and archeological fields of Utah. Hollis had discovered an entire graveyard of dinosaur bones in Utah, but her project ran out of money and the rancher who owned the land didn't really care for people digging around his property and made life miserable for her every chance he got. That, coupled with the lack of funding forced her to abandon the project so she could go make money just to live on.

She and Gail had been roommates all through college at the University of Texas and never once had an argument about anything. They were truly kindred spirits and enjoyed life together. They remained roommates as they both pursued their Doctorate's in Geology and Archeology. They were currently being paid by the owners of the Dynamic Bridge Caverns near San Antonio to map more of the cave that had yet to be explored. The cave was relatively new in terms of being discovered in the 60's. There wasn't anything special about the cave, but it was a tourist attraction and it was beautiful. Most would consider the twelve-dollar price of admission worth the money. Gail and Hollis were getting pretty much free reign of the place after and during visitation hours. The pay was pretty good, and they had uncovered some new caverns that made the ones seen by the public look like a closet. The owners were certain to make a killing once they made it safe for tourism. "We can't go that way, Gail, we were given specific instructions to stay clear of the West corridors." Gail ignored the conversation and turned West. The beam of her headlamp disappeared as she headed West. Hollis was used to these little excursions and some had even been helpful, but this time Gail didn't return. "Gail!" She called out with no return call, which was strictly against their self-developed code of exploration. She let out a sigh then started in the direction that Gail had headed.

Every step of the way she called for Gail but got no response. The tunnel that headed West was quite narrow and it was possible that the echo and reverberation would never reach Gail. Caves did tricky things sometimes. Hollis heard the very soft whisper of her name and she froze. She was certain it was

Gail, but she couldn't see her. "Switch off your lamp and be very still." Hollis did not like games and often Gail liked to try to scare her. "Dang it, Gail, we don't have time for this." She waited for a reply which came later than what Hollis considered proper dialogue. The faint whisper came again. "Please be quiet and switch off your headlamp. Don't take another step forward." This time Hollis froze; there was something in Gail's voice that she had never heard before, nervousness. She switched off her headlamp as instructed. It took a few minutes for her eyes to adjust to the dark. She thought it would be pitch black, but it wasn't. When her eyes adjusted, Hollis could see that she and Gail were standing on a ledge and there was a green phosphorous glow coming from way beneath them, but she could also see a red glow of what looked like an outline of a door just a few feet ahead of them. "I am going to edge over to the outline of the door – I didn't want to fall off this ledge before you caught up to me, then you would never know what happened to me." Hollis was having trouble breathing; it felt like she was breathing Sulphur, which could be deadly. "Gail, don't you dare go that way. We don't get paid enough to take risks like this! I don't like this place one bit at all!" Gail hit the outline of the door. The screech came and they both entered the red outlined door like being sucked into a vacuum. Once inside, there was light, and the green glow was no longer beneath them. They were standing in an open room, adorned with markings that both were familiar with. The pictographs were early Native American, very early.

They knew they had made a real find and were excited beyond belief. Hollis began examining all the symbols and drawings that seemed to cover the entire room from ceiling to floor. It was difficult to decipher but she started calling out the symbols as she recognized them: Sun, Fire, Earth, Rain, Moon, and each time she called them out loud the room changed, shifted, a phosphorus style glow would flash a different vibrant color or the room shook and rumbled. She got to the symbol for Wind and Gail screamed for Hollis to stop but it was too late. They didn't realize it at the time but they had unleashed forces that they were ill prepared to deal with. Before either could speak to the other they disappeared.

Chapter 2

SHE HIT THE SNOOZE BUTTON one more time. She lay there in the suit that God had given her. Pure nakedness in bed just felt weird without him. She enjoyed that feeling she got when he was there; he snores like grizzly bear in the first month of hibernation, but she didn't mind. Once he had her wrapped up in his death grip embrace, he wouldn't move the entire night. Seemed odd at first since most guys don't snuggle but he was different. He seemed to pick up energy from it.

The night had been a fun one hanging out with the gang, maybe a bit too fun. Her head started pounding the minute she stood up and made her way to bathroom. She had done shots with the other chicks while the boys were on a run. Way too many shots because not only did her head pound, her stomach was having its own intestinal Olympics and the judges were not happy with its performance. It was rare that it was just the women, but they took advantage of it. She was the toughest of all of them. In fact, if she thought long enough she could remember the time she had beaten the hell out of all of them, one at a time, of course, but it was for certain that they all knew to a stay clear of him. A few new ones had batted the wrong eye towards him and they had paid the price.

She didn't carry a grudge long, but she could remember every cracked tooth, black eye, and broken finger. She was very dainty when she was growing up, but he had somehow changed her. He made her tougher, smarter, and when she was with him, she knew she was the only woman on the planet. At least that is the way he made her feel. After all, he was the Boss.

But before she dressed... a hot shower was in order. The Boss...just the thought of him made her tingle. He had a way of driving her crazy when she was with him and even more crazy when he was away. Where was he now, she wondered?

Chapter 3

"HOLY HELL! LOOK AT THAT!" he said as he pointed toward the Northern sky. The Boss and his crew were headed West on I-40 just West of Amarillo when he saw what looked like the biggest thunder cloud he had ever seen. His mind imagined that it was about to give birth to a tornado. He'd had wind in his hair his whole life, basically. His first memories were of a Radio Flyer he used to fly off the side of a ravine near the house his step-dad had moved them to in Southern Mississippi when he was just 6.

It really wasn't a house, more like a sharecropper shack that he paid dirt-cheap rent to a former plantation owner just for the privilege of living in a place where nobody could hear him smack his mother around when he got drunk or did that thing with a needle and a spoon. The Boss swore he'd never hit a woman as long as he lived, and he also swore that when he was old enough, he'd end the beatings his momma took from that creep of a step-dad. At first, he refused to call the creep "dad" but when he wouldn't do it and "Ace" was full of moonshine, he'd twist his mother's arm behind her back until she begged her only son to call him "daddy". He hated the son of a bitch for sure but his stepdad "Ace" eventually would have to answer for his behavior from the Boss. Those bad memories always brought him back to reality and it also brought him back to the problem at hand. He needed to get his crew off this highway before they all ended up in Kansas wearing striped socks like that Witch.

He motioned to an underpass and they all trailed in behind him. You could hear the roar for miles as each bike engine echoed off the walls of the underpass. He dropped the kickstand and switched off the key to his 46 Knucklehead. Besides his old lady, this bike was all he cared about in this world. If he could tote that prize to the top of this underpass he would, but for now, he'd have to take his chances and hope that this Texas titty twister wouldn't grab it and take it to Kansas without him.

"Jack – you get the saddlebags, without those this trip is a waste. Get every-one up this slope. I want everyone wedged in as tight as your fat asses will wedge. Grab the next man's arm, or leg, I don't give a shit what you grab but by god if this son of bitch takes one of us, it's going to take us all. I mean it!" Everyone knew he meant it. The Boss didn't look like much; pull the club colors off him and slap one of those Wall Street suits on him and you'd never know the Boss was a bad dude.

Jack Ingle was his right-hand man. He was excellent under pressure and the Boss counted on him. Jack was tough as nails and as far as Paul knew, wasn't scared of anything or anyone. He trusted him explicitly because of what had become known as the fight. It was epic for anyone who was there to tell about it.

Only a few in the fight were left standing at the end. The walls were covered in blood and still smoking from bullet holes when the cops got there. At the time, Jack was a strong lieutenant on the rise and the Boss was nothing more than a "prospect". The story had it that Jack was simply supposed to make an exchange of "cash for hash" as they used to call it back in the day. Jack walked into the bar with his prospect there to learn the ropes when a man named Bolton, a very bad man showed up. It was totally unexpected and the Boss, as young as he was back then, knew something was wrong and some bad shit was about to go down.

Bolton was a rival that had stones the size of watermelons and the brains of a retarded gnat. For reasons folks still can't explain, Bolton sucker-punched Jack on the exchange of cash for hash. The punch broke Jack's jaw and nose and left him unconscious on the floor. Apparently, Bolton wanted the cash and the hash and as it turned out, with Jack sprawled out on that floor, the prospect ended up one-on-one with the big Neanderthal. After the Neanderthal and prospect exchanged several haymakers and destroyed the entire bar, the story goes that the Boss hit Bolton in the throat with the bottom of a beer bottle so hard that it shattered in the process, severing Bolton's carotid artery. It was clearly self-defense, at least that is what the lawyer said at the trial.

When they finally bailed the Boss out of jail 4 days later, he was still covered in blood spatter. He had refused to remove the blood because he saw it as an opportunity to build a legacy, so he wanted everyone to see he was a bad man. It must have worked because after that fight, he was no longer a prospect. He was full-on member. And even better, he was respected.

Chapter 4

SHE STOOD IN FRONT OF THE MIRROR for an especially long time this morning. She was never much on mirrors, she knew she was attractive and really didn't need to work at it. She took care of herself, ate right, and exercised; all the shit a woman should do. She even enjoyed the exercise. She could out-work girls half her age. She once took one of those resistance work out classes where there isn't much weight lifting, just where you use your own body weight against itself and it tones your muscles. She took an entire year of classes and she could actually see her stomach muscles. She was very proud of what she had done. But when he finally stopped long enough and saw her stomach muscles, he actually crinkled his nose.

He told her that she was all woman just the way she was and didn't need that six-pack shit. He told her no woman on the planet turned him on more than she did. He might not have been a wordsmith when it came to charming people, but she knew what he meant. He had a way of making her feel like she was the most beautiful woman in the room. She would do anything for him for that very reason alone. He was always genuine with her. She stood in front of the mirror longer this morning because she wanted to send him a selfie. She didn't do it often, but she wanted to badly this morning. In fact, she felt an overwhelming compulsion to do it. It was like he was pulling at her subconscious from wherever he was and was begging her to enter into his.

She put on his favorite black skirt with a soft peach blouse. She smiled when she was buttoning the blouse, remembering that nearly every single time he saw it on her, he ended up unbuttoning it and removing it from her very slowly. She loved it, the way he would stare into her eyes as his hands softly untangled each button. He never looked away from her eyes; his hands just figured it out. Sometimes she would have to remind herself to breathe. She slid a pair of black pumps on her well- pedicured feet. A true source of pride for her.

He loved her feet too! He would spend hours sitting on the couch rubbing her feet. He would tell her not to tell the boys he was such a pushover when it came to taking care of her beautiful feet. The black heels were his second favorite shoes she wore. He loved the cream heels, but they didn't quite go well with the black skirt, so they would have to do. She smiled again, remembering the time she turned him on so much in these shoes that he wouldn't let her take them off the entire time he was making love to her.

God, she missed him. She hated these "runs". He always came back with a new scar, a black eye, broken ribs, or something that required her magical touch. But he always came back to her and he always came back with a pile of cash. She never asked a question, that wasn't her role. Her role, as far as she was concerned, was to keep him happy and healthy. She was good at it.

Chapter 5

EACHMAN WAS LOCKED IN ARMS at the highest point of the underpass. They wedged themselves in as tightly as they could. The pressure around them was intense. His ears began to pop. He could hardy hear but he knew it was damn loud. Little pieces of gravel pelted him. He wondered how in the hell he was getting hit with gravel when he was jammed so far up into this underpass. His clothes flapped even though he knew the jacket and jeans he had on were a pretty snug fit. If this thing didn't end soon he was sure he would be squatting here naked. He didn't dare open his eyes for fear he would lose them with all this gravel pelting him. He just kept a death grip on the two riders that were next to him. Damn, it stung.

It couldn't have lasted more than a couple minutes, but it seemed like an hour. When he could hear again, he squinted his eyes open slowly. He cracked a James Dean when he realized it wasn't gravel that had been tearing at his clothes and exposed skin, it was frickin' hay. Hay, like the damn cows eat, was being shot through the air at such velocity that it was about to rip the clothes and flesh right off him. Geez, that tornado was a bad piece of luck all right. He tried to let go of the men he was hanging on to but realized they weren't there. Fact was, nobody was there. He looked down at what was left of I-40 and realized there were no bikes either.

His 46 Knucklehead was nowhere to be found. He needed to find his boys. Fuck that, he needed to find Michele. Michele was his name for the bike. He had it painted a few years back on the tank. It was a beautiful two- tone metallic paint job that he had done by one of the best paint guys in all of Texas. The problem was, the paint guy wasn't very bright and had left off one of the L's in her name. Paul started to have him redo it but after thinking through it, he liked it. Thus, the new nickname for the bike was "Stingy L" now. Michele was missing and so were the saddlebags. He needed to find them. That became very urgent. How far can a tornado toss 30 bikes and 29 guys, he wondered? He didn't know, but his dingoes started moving before his mind could. He had never done business with these cats, but they didn't seem like the type to give a flip-flying fuck about natural disasters or his starring role in this creepy version of The Wizard of Oz. That farmhouse was not going to fall on him. No fucking way. He set out to find the bike, the bags, and hopefully scoop up a few of his men. He wasn't a praying man either, but he knew if those saddlebags broke open, it wouldn't matter what he thought or what the camel jockeys thought. He wasn't completely certain what the contents were but he assumed, based off what they were paying him it was some high-quality shit.

Chapter 6

SHE SNAPPED A SELFIE THEN checked it to see if she was pleased with it and, of course, she wasn't. She snapped 4 more, each with slightly different poses; one leg out, head cocked to one side. She finally settled on a nice smile with her left foot sort of in front of the other. She liked the way she looked and knew he would too. She uploaded the picture to the message, typed in "All yours", and hit "Send".

The selfie never got to him. His ears were still popping from the sudden air compression. He tried to yawn; that didn't work so he pinched his nose shut, closed his mouth, and blew. That worked. His ears were clear again. He slid down the overpass ramp until he reached the road. The weirdest thing was that after all that wind and rain, it was currently sunny and calm. He had no idea how that happened, but he was grateful it was clear now. He looked both East and West along the highway and could see the path the tornado had taken. It clearly had moved from North to South as it ripped up a swath of Interstate 40 about a mile wide. Weren't going to be any interstate commerce passing through this part of West Texas for a while.

There was debris for as far as he could see. Somehow the force of the swirling wind had oddly stacked what seemed to be a complete herd of cows in a nice tidy pyramid. He guessed there were probably 50 cows in the ancient formation. He laughed out loud. "I could live another 50 years and not see anything like that." At least the owner won't have any trouble rounding them up. The tornado had done the wrangling for him. He was having a lot of personal laughs at the expense of all these potential steaks when he spotted a leg sticking up out of the now flattened rows of corn. The word "shit" came slowly and softly out of his mouth. He heard himself say it but never really meant to say it out loud. He had seen dead bodies in his line of work; he had actually been the cause of several of them taking their last breaths. The dead leg didn't bother him as much as the age; this was a child's leg, maybe toddler years. Hell, he didn't guess ages very well. He approached the leg with a slight amount of reluctance. Dead thugs from a different tribe was one thing but seeing a dead baby made him uneasy.

As he approached the leg, it moved. He stopped cold in his tracks. Maybe he had just imagined it moved so he stood still long enough to see the little toes twitch. Then he heard it. He heard a screech that made his skin crawl. It wasn't human, and it wasn't an animal, but it was definitely close. Something in his instincts told him he needed to move quickly so he took three quick steps and found himself standing over a little girl covered in dirt and corn and she was bleeding from her forehead. She seemed to be asleep, or at peace, but when her eyes opened and met his, she screamed the scream that little girls do when they've seen a spider, which caused him to step back. He gave her what he thought was enough distance to put her at ease, but it didn't seem to work because she continued to scream. After her vocal cords started to play out on her, the screams turned to a steady whimper. "Pipe down, little girl. You're ok." He said it with his same Boss biker voice and realized at that very moment he had zero experience with a baby goo goo voice that his brother had. He used to make fun of his brother for being such a pussy. His gruffness in address scared her even more, it seemed, so he tried to soften his words a little and said, "Baby girl – it's going to be ok. You need to come with me, so we can maybe find your parents." Then came the screech again, only this time closer. It was seriously time to move.

Chapter 7

RENEE GRABBED HER PURSE and keys and headed out the door. She was definitely a working woman, always had been. She was good at her job and she actually liked it. Her dad used to complain about work all the time. He worked for the same car dealership for over 40 years before he retired. He was consistent in his approach to life though: show up, be on time, do a good job, and take care of your family. Nowhere did it ever occur to him to change jobs. He grew up in an era that generally told us all that we should be happy that we had a job.

She bounced around a few jobs in her lifetime but never felt as loyal to one as she was to this one. She had even been fired twice and both times proved to be life-altering and unjustified. She was a nice-looking woman, for sure, and that seemed to cause issues at the places she worked. The first time she was fired was when she worked for Barnett-Hackney Construction as a construction coordinator for corporate projects. She dealt with all the big shots of major corporations and was never intimidated by titles or a thousand-dollar pair of shoes. She liked the job but her direct supervisor was a dick. She and all the other ladies at the company quietly referred to him as a "fuck stick" but the girls had several nicknames for the jerk.

He hit on her constantly. Even arranged "scouting" trips that just the two of them were scheduled for overnight. She finally got fed up with it and complained to the HR Department and to her surprise, she was fired just two weeks after she registered the compliant. Her reason for termination was "inability to perform job". She knew the only job she didn't have the ability to perform in that firm was the blowjob her direct supervisor was constantly begging for. At first, she was pissed, but it occurred to her that this turn of events might work in her favor.

Everyone in the company knew that the prick she was working for spent most of his time trying to yank down the panties of every woman in the company. If she took them to court, she figured there would be too many people who would be afraid of perjury and would have to state on the witness stand that indeed "Johnny Appleseed", one of his other nicknames around the firm, had in fact hit on many others besides her. She was right. The Barnett-Hackney suits decided it best to settle out of court. After her lawyer fees were paid, she walked away from the lawsuit with a cool quarter of a million dollars. Not bad for a woman who just turned 30.

The second place she was fired from was a medical supply firm. She was responsible for sales of equipment used in the operating room. Although this job paid her handsomely, she really hated this job. It seemed like the people who made all the purchase decisions for the hospital looked down on you. She was a college graduate with a degree in Economics from Southern Methodist University in Dallas. She also had a Master's in Business from Tulane University, which is where she first met the Boss on Bourbon Street in New Orleans; she smiled when she thought about that chance encounter with him. Anyway, it didn't seem to matter to the hospital pencil necks. They all thought she was just a dumb broad who sold scalpels for a living. Despite how her clients saw her, she was a top salesman. She had all the company awards to prove it. Even though she stood 5'7" with great legs and a body that could stop a train, the certificates and plaques all read "sales-MAN". Whatever...the job paid well, and she enjoyed the travel. She was fired from that job for supposedly falsifying her travel expense vouchers. What a load of shit that was.

She was a meticulous record keeper and had never falsified anything in her life. The real story was that the horny doctor at Mercy General tried to shove her into a supply closet for a quickie. She easily fended him off with a knee to the groin and as he was deciding at that very moment if he should be a man or a woman all hunched over in pain, she delivered a nifty uppercut to the chin and he crumpled like yesterday's laundry. What a pussy, she thought. Luckily, as the trial played out, it was all caught on camera; the actual shove into the closet and, this was the kicker, the hospital had installed a camera inside that same closet because apparently, it became a haven for horny interns, staff, and nurses.

The place seemed to be a haven for discarded condoms that the geniuses happily tossed into a corner as some sort of monument to their conquest. The custodial staff took exception to the practice and reported it to the administration. Thus, the cameras. And they looked down on her? What morons. They would still be banging away in the broom closet if they had simply been smart enough to toss their spent "shell casings" in the trash and not in the corner. The jury was out for just thirty minutes before they returned a wrongful termination verdict and after attorney's fees, awarded her another quarter million dollars.

That award was just part of it. She also sued Mercy General and with the video evidence fresh on their minds, they decided to settle rather quickly. It was considered an undisclosed sum but after attorney's fees, she walked away from that settlement with 1.7 million. Apparently, the attempted rape charges added to their Chief of Staff's resume was frowned upon. She didn't care, she was barely 30 and now she was a millionaire, no worse for the wear.

Chapter 8

PAUL AKA "THE BOSS" yanked the corn stalks away from the little girl, reached down into the little hole that had obviously provided her with enough shelter to save her life, and lifted her into his arms. The squeal made him skittish enough that he wasn't overly concerned about how gentle he was with the girl. He held her under his arm like a football. He honestly couldn't remember if he had ever in his life picked up a kid. He didn't think so, but this seemed to be a day of firsts for everything. He needed to find his 46 and the saddlebags and get moving. Since to his left was nothing but torn up I-40 and flatlands as far as he could see, he figured the bikes must have been lifted and tossed somewhere in the tree line. The footing was difficult because the field seemed as though it had just been plowed, so with each step he sank just enough to feel off-balance, so he started making more hops than strides until he reached the tree line and was out of the corn field.

Once he made the tree line and saw that the woods weren't quite as thick as what he thought, he started to see pieces of bike parts. As he was looking for anything or pieces that might resemble his 46, he tripped. He still had the little girl under his arm. His instincts spun his body under the girl so he wouldn't land on her, but when he was falling and twisting, he lost sight of the ground. He felt the sudden shooting pain in his left shoulder and then a smashing pain just above his left ear, which sent him out like a light. "Down goes Frazier" was his last thought....

He blinked as he tried to bring focus back to his eyes that were now blurry and watery. He figured watery was a good sign as that meant he was just briefly knocked out. He could feel hands on his face but with the blurry vision he couldn't quite make out who was touching him. He could hear someone's voice, but everything was muffled. Reality started to come back when the hands that gently cupped his face now turned into malicious tiny little pinchers.

She pinched both of his cheeks like her daddy used to do to her to make her get up. It wasn't a hard pinch. In the morning her daddy would put two hands on her cheeks, kiss her fore-head, then playfully pinch both of her cheeks and say, "Wake up, princess, it's time to take on the world!" She was usually already awake when her daddy would come in, but she would keep her eyes closed really tightly so they could play the game every morning. She knew there was nothing like her daddy; he was big and strong, and he was her protector. He had to be close by because she remembered holding his hand in the storm cellar. She remembered that he had gotten up to check the latch on the storm door because it was shaking so badly that dust was coming in through the tiny cracks and stinging her face. And the noise! Oh, the noise was so loud she couldn't hear anything he was saying and then all the sudden, he was gone. He had to be close by though. They had just been holding hands, she thought, and she had to wake this man up so he could help her find her daddy.

"Ouch! Motherfucker! That hurts! You need to clip those nails, kid! Am I bleeding now?" He looked up at the girl. She was sitting on his chest with both hands still on his cheeks so hard that they smashed his lips together and made home look like a fish. His vision came back quickly after the pinch test. The little girl had the most beautiful blue eyes he had ever seen. "My daddy doesn't say motherfucker, what does that mean?" she asked. "Does it mean you are awake and ready to take on the world?" She looked firmly into his eyes and then leaned in so close to his face that he could see the weird little designs in the pupils of her eyes. "Because that's what my daddy says every morning when he wakes up. I say it too." He laid his head back down on the ground to give himself a little space from the kid's face. "No, that's not what it means, and you shouldn't ever say it." She got a puzzled look on her face as she looked around the forest. "Then why do you say it if I can't say it?" "Because it's a word only grown-ups use, not little girls who play with Barbies." "My daddy is a grown up and he doesn't say it." Got me there, he thought. I am lying on my back, I have a throbbing headache, lost my crew and my bike, and now I am matching wits with a 6-year old. Well Happy fucking Christmas...

"My name is Ariel, just like in the movies and coloring books. What's your name, mister? I like to color, I have lots of crayons, my daddy says there are 64 in the box but he doesn't know I've added 5 new colors that weren't in the box before. That makes 69 colors. Can you count like me? I'm good at it. My daddy says I am a genius. I don't know exactly what that means but I think it means I can add and subtract really fast. Do you like to color? You must like to color a lot. My favorite color is yellow. My daddy named me after the mermaid, but she isn't my favorite, my favorite is Belle. You know who Belle is? She is a princess and she wears yellow clothes all the time and every day of the week! She is beautiful. My daddy says I am beautiful. I don't know if I am or not, I look in the mirror and I just see me. I don't see anything real beautiful. I especially don't see Belle. She is beautiful. Did you say you like to color? I know that I get in trouble when I color on my skin or clothes though. You have colored all over both your arms. Some of the pictures are really pretty and some are really scary. You have a skeleton just like I wore last year for Halloween when I was little, but it wasn't a scary skeleton like yours, mine was a happy skeleton. You shouldn't draw boobies on your skin either. It's not right to draw boobies any-where, especially on an angel. How do you know that angels have boobies anyway? Can you help me find my daddy, mis-ter? I am kinda scared."

My God how many questions can come out of one person in less than a minute? His head really hurt now. Was he supposed to respond to all those questions? What is conversational eti-quette for children? He had no idea. His first inclination was to tell this little noise maker to shut the fuck up but that would probably make her spit out a host of new and more confus-ing questions. "Yes, I will help you find your daddy if you help me find my bike, but I can't do it with you sitting on my chest." She leaped off him like she had just set off a mouse-trap. She stood beside him holding his hand until he regained his footing and was able to shake the cobwebs out of his head enough to maintain upright balance. She squeezed his hand as he heard the screech again, but it seemed a little more distant.

Chapter 9

RENEE HIT THE LIGHT SWITCH as she walked out through the garage door. When she touched the switch, an immediate jolt went from her index finger then shot to her funny bone which caused her hand to go numb; the pain was immediate and intense. That was all she could remember. She woke up on the garage floor looking up at the ceiling. At first, she had no idea how she got there. She rolled to one side to help aid in sitting upright, but when she put her right elbow on the ground as a temporary prop, she screamed in pain. She looked down and realized that she had a hole in the back of her elbow. It looked perfectly round and burnt around the edges. She had read somewhere that when electricity decides to exit your body; it does not deliver a cordial goodbye. It lets you know its power as it exits. That must be what happened.

She remembered the shock. She looked up and could see that the light switch was burnt to a crisp. What the hell? She had lived in this house for 10 years – hell, she had it built, and it never had so much as a leaky faucet. She managed to roll to her other side, using her good arm to help push her way back to upright. When she finally stood, she felt very dizzy and thought she might pass out again, so she stepped toward her workbench to steady herself. As she was shaking out the dizziness, she felt the rush of last night's party come roaring up from her stomach.

She dumped what was left of the tequila shooters and sliders all over her garage floor. Gross! I hate throwing up...As she was heaving-up the last of Jose, she heard the screech. It sent chills down her spine. The hair on her arms started their own electrical storm, standing straight up. Jesus – what was that? She smiled for a second as she realized she was whispering to no one. The screech came again so loud that she was dead certain it was coming from right outside her garage. Ok, she thought. I don't scare easily but I sure wish Paul were here. She tiptoed back into her house careful not to touch any electrical switches. She continued to tiptoe, she wasn't exactly sure why she was tiptoeing, but something in her head was telling her to be quiet and unseen. With all the quietness and stealth, she could summon with her current dizzy and nauseated stomach, she headed straight for her nightstand.

Her favorite crime stopper was always faithfully waiting to help when the alarm bells went off. She eased the drawer open quietly and extracted her nickel plated .45. It was a double stack and had some "heft" to it when fully loaded but she was more than capable of handling it. She had a concealed permit in 9 states, including New York and Connecticut, two of the toughest states to obtain permits. As quietly as she could, she jacked a round in the chamber but kept the safety on.

Chapter 10

"MISTER, WHERE IS MY DADDY?" She squeezed his hand as she was speaking. "What is that noise? I don't like it, it sounds mean." He looked around the strand of trees and surveyed the spot where he had fallen and cracked his head. He realized that he had tripped on handlebars that were sticking out of the ground. He knew they were motorcycle handlebars, but he also knew they weren't his 46. Geez – why is a motorcycle buried in the ground and if this has happened because of that tornado, maybe his was buried too? How the hell could he dig out a motorcycle? He needed to send his angel a message to let her know he was in a jam, but his phone was in the saddlebags.

He sat up straight and rubbed his forehead. It was an ample forehead. His close friends would joke that his forehead was so big that he must have been a "five head". The thought of the joke made him chuckle a little. "Did you say your name was Ariel?" He reached under her arm and moved her off his lap so he could get up. As he was getting up he noticed a flash of metal in a tree a few yards away from where he was. He gently got up – his back was sore for sure. "I wish I knew where your old man was kid because I would sure like him to take you back."

When he stood his legs wobbled a little bit and Ariel must have noticed because she grabbed his hand and tried to help steady his wobbly legs. At first Paul didn't catch the gesture but he realize that it was probably not normal for a child so small to try and steady someone twice her size. She was quickly finding a spot in his heart and there was nothing he could do to prevent that from happening.

Chapter 11

SHE DREW A BREATH TO STEADY her stomach, but she caught a whiff of her own vomit at the moment she drew in her breath. The rush of foulness made her wretch again but this time there was nothing left to heave up. She felt her stomach spasm as if it were in complete control of her entire body. Sweat popped up on her forehead as she made the promise she had made several times in her life, I am NEVER drinking again.

She went to the circuit breaker box and reset the breaker that had blown. The lights in the garage came back on immediately. Her heart raced as she was preparing to meet the "screech" with her .45 if necessary. She felt the pain in her elbow as she raised the .45 in tandem with the garage door opening.

As the outside sunshine flooded the once dimly-lit garage, nothing lurched toward her as she had fully expected, nothing but the calmness of the morning. She decided she needed a full view and stepped out onto the driveway. Again, nothing.

She surveyed the entire scene, she looked to the right and left of the house but saw nothing unusual. A squirrel scampered up a tree in the neighbor's yard but that was about it. She never noticed the eyes peering at her.

She clicked the safety on her .45 as she lowered it to her side. She still wanted to know where that screech was coming from but at the moment, it was silent. She decided she needed to attend to her elbow as it was throbbing with pain now that her adrenaline wore off. She closed the garage and headed for the kitchen where she kept the medicine and Band-Aids, although she thought she would need more than just a Band-Aid. There was a freaking burned out hole in the back of her arm. She needed to go to the doctor to get checked and stitched up.

Despite the pain, she cleaned the back of her elbow as best she could. She wrapped it in some gauze and taped it well enough that it restricted her bending her elbow. She felt it was good enough for now until she could see Dr. Dresnek. Dr. Dresnek had been her family doctor as long as she could remember. He was a good man with a soft demeanor. He always looked at you when he talked to you; he spoke to you on your terms, not medical terms. He would shake your hand when he first saw you and shake your hand when he was finished. He had the softest hands of anyone she had ever met. He made you feel important and she liked that. Yep, she thought. I am going to go see Dr. Dresnek.

Chapter 12

"JIM, YOU HAVE TO UNDERSTAND, damn it. That was no accident, that was a transformative man-made event. We didn't just have some kind of weather "event" in 165 separate locations from Texas to Montana and say it was caused by some freak accident of nature?" He used air quotes with his fingers when he said event. "It just doesn't add up, Jim." Mark Dresnek was President Jim Stafford's closest friend and Chief of Staff. He was given a little more latitude than others to address the President of the United States in such a harsh tone.

They had been friends since they were little boys. Both grew up in West Texas. Jim's dad was an oil man, not the kind that lit cigars with 100- dollar bills, no, he started as a tool pusher, roughneck, and worked his way up through the ranks at Bloomfield Drilling Company. He was a hard- working man, no-nonsense in every aspect of the business, but he also had a giant heart. He would give anyone a chance on his rigs. It didn't matter if you were in trouble or had a record or just out of prison, he would extend the same hand to them that he would extend to the president of the company.

Status mattered very little to Jim Stafford Senior. He was killed in a drilling explosion when Jim Stafford Jr. was in high school. He wasn't even supposed to be at the drilling site but there had been an emergency and they couldn't reach the location foreman, so he rose from his family dinner that night, told everyone he'd be back in a few hours, grabbed his hard hat, and headed out. That was the last time Jim Jr. ever saw his dad. Mark's dad, the doctor, sort of took on the father role after the accident. You might even say it was Dr. Dresnek who helped Jim Stafford launch his political career by helping him get into Yale University. It was at Yale that Jim Jr. developed friendships and connections that would serve him all the way to the highest office in the land. Both Jim Jr. and Mark attended Yale, but Mark was supposed to follow in his dad's footsteps and become a doctor, but Mark had no stomach for blood. He nearly passed out at the sight of it. Instead, he went into law and actually became a very good trial lawyer while he was assigned to the District Attorney's office in Dallas, Texas.

He was considered a brawler in the courtroom. He pushed the limits on courtroom etiquette and often found himself in contempt. He always seemed to know where the line in the sand was with each judge and he pushed it right up to that line quite often. When he was the Assistant DA he was assigned the prosecution of 11 South Dallas gang members. These were not thugs, they were very organized in the drug trafficking business and were connected to the mob. They ruled almost all South Dallas with absolute fear.

Despite two separate attempts on his life, he managed to convict all 11 on racketeering, extortion, and even got three of them convicted for murder. It was a tense time, but Mark was admired for his grit and toughness in not backing down when he clearly could have, and some say he should have. When Jim became Governor of Texas, he asked his best friend if he would become his chief of staff and legal advisor. There wasn't much of a discussion. Mark took the job without blinking.

"What do you want me to do, where do I direct the drone strikes, buddy?" He ran his hand through his hair as he contemplated his next steps. "I get your point that it isn't a freak of nature but hell, we don't know why there were all those tornadoes all at once. We have no satellite readings that are out of line; our jets are scrambled and report absolutely nothing but calm at the moment. There are no suspicious border crossings as of late, NSA has picked up absolutely ZERO (he made an "OK" zero with his left hand for dramatic effect even though he knew he didn't need theatrics with Mark) internet chatter suggestions that terrorists had anything to do with this, the only thing abnormal is people all over the country are reporting a screeching sound. They say it sounds like a wounded animal or something like heavy metal plates rubbing against each other." Jim paced the Oval Office from wall to wall. He had always been known for thinking on his feet, but he was stumped on this one. "Have you asked for Dobson yet?"

Annemarie Dobson was the Chairman of the Joint Chiefs of Staff. She was the first female Navy Seal, first woman allowed in combat, and was one of the very few female congressional Medal of Honor winners. She was tough, smart, and was actually quite beautiful. Mark always got butterflies around her. He loved to hear her talk, he loved to watch how she commanded a room and how she could gracefully go from being a bad ass four-star general to a graceful, beautiful woman. He never let anyone know how she made him feel. Not even his best friend. Even though he was single, and she was widowed, there would be nothing prohibiting him from asking her out on a date, he just always seemed to feel a little inferior around her. She was that well put together.

"Yes, she is on her way here now, she was at Aviano checking out the base there and offering some diplomatic solutions to the Prime Minister." Mark chuckled at that because he knew what "diplomatic solutions" she was offering. She was in Italy to rip the PM's ass over his comments about women in combat and reminded him that the U.S. had stuck by him when he got caught cheating with a 19-year-old staffer. She was good at that stuff.

"We had a Raptor pick her up at super-sonic and put her in a little uncomfortable flight suit and she should be here in about an hour." "You stuck her on a Raptor?" Mark smiled when he said it and thought to himself, lucky pilot. Single cockpit and very little room but one of the fastest planes we had available over there. "How the hell do two people fit in a Raptor cockpit?" Mark asked out loud. "Don't ask me but the pilot said he could do it and he would have her here within the hour." Mark drew in a breath to steady himself before he spoke. "You want to call a cabinet meeting?" Jim was standing behind his desk when Ellen, the President's Oval Office secretary, came over the speaker: "Mr. President – the chairwoman is here now, would you like me to send her in?" Mark immediately tensed up. He reached in his pocket for breath spray and realized he didn't have any so he thought it would be safe if he would just shake hands at a nice comfortable distance and not get too close to her. He had garlic toast for lunch and knew that she would be able to smell it. "Yes, Ellen, please." "Man, those Air Force fly boys really know how to drop the hammer. She is 30 minutes ahead of schedule."

Chapter 13

THE LITTLE GIRL TOOK A STEP BACK, just enough to give him room to stand up but never let go of his hand. "Yes!" She proclaimed loudly as if he had just answered the secret tea question of the day. "Just like the mermaid!" Paul stood there looking down at this beautiful little girl holding his hand and chattering like those fake wind-up teeth you buy at a gag store. She absolutely would not stop talking. He thought to himself, today I started out in bed with the most beautiful woman in the world, got on my Knucklehead, and headed West to deliver some high quality "stuff" to some cats in Denver. He had never met them, but they were willing to pay him more money than he had ever made in his life to deliver the "stuff", enough money that he would never have to work again. He had no idea what the "stuff" was, he never asked questions like that. He was just the moving company. The contents of the cargo wasn't his business.

The only real question he asked was could he go to jail if he were caught with it. In this case, they were emphatic that he could not go to jail, but he needed to be overly cautious in the way it was handled. He always was cautious, barring tornadoes. He felt good about the day and now here he was, on foot, holding hands with a five-year old girl who is named after a mermaid. Life sure takes some weird turns. "Yes, you told me, just like the mermaid but you'd rather be Belle. I have a pretty good memory, kid." She smiled at him and before he realized it, he had cracked a smile back at her.

He shook his head a little to see if there were any cobwebs left from the fall. He was clear. He had complete control of himself again. He looked around to locate that metal flash he saw in the trees right before he fell. He didn't locate it but decided that it was time to start moving. As best he could figure, he was just South of Amarillo somewhere, so he should just point himself North and start walking. He figured they would eventually run into a farmhouse or someone who could help them with a phone or something. He was still internally cursing himself for putting his damn cell phone in the saddlebags instead of keeping it in his vest pocket.

Ariel was looking around as if she was Alice in Wonderland and for all he knew, they very well could be. He was screwed. Didn't even have his 45 with him, it too, was in the saddlebags. Rookie mistake for sure. "Mister, do you think we can find my daddy?" He was about to answer when the little chatter box started her rapid-fire questions: Mister – what kind of tree is that? It's big, I can climb trees. I am a good climber. I got in trouble one time because I climbed up so high in a tree in our back yard that I couldn't figure out how to get down. My daddy had to climb up and get me, but he got stuck too. My mommy had to call a fire truck and they helped us get down. It was so fun! They had the lights on their big red truck going and all the neighbors came out to watch. The man that climbed up the ladder to get me, oh— and my daddy was real nice. He picked me up and held me real tight. His coat was real scratchy though. It hurt. I told him he needed a softer coat, but he said he liked the one he had. And, he said the one he had couldn't catch on fire and it helped him do his job better. I still think he should get a softer coat." Paul let out a breath of frustration, "Ariel – do you know how to play the quiet game?" Paul could think of no other trick to get her be quiet while they walked.

He just had this uneasy feeling that they were being watched. He hadn't seen anyone and had no reason to feel that way, but in most situations, he trusted his gut. In this case, he needed her to be quiet for just a few precious minutes so he could listen to his surroundings. Unfortunately, Ariel's answer shut the door on that idea. "I do but I am not good at it. My daddy wins every time we play because I like to talk. There is so much to see and talk about that I just don't understand why anyone would want to be quiet." He strained to hear through her chatter. He thought he could hear talking in the distance or what sounded like talking from a distance. Maybe it was just Ariel's consistent jabbering that reverberated off the inside walls of his head now. If only she had an off switch he would have flipped it an hour ago.

Ariel was talking about how much she liked to spend time at her cousin's house because her cousin was a boy and he had the neatest toys. She really liked all her Barbies but she said she needed a break from girl toys every now and then when Paul heard the unmistakable sound of a hammer being cocked. He was weighing his options and pretending not to notice that he had heard anything. He knew he had nothing in the way of defense for himself and Ariel and was pretty much shit out of luck when he heard a voice. "Mister – I don't mean you any harm but I am locked and loaded so when you turn around don't do anything stupid or I will drop you like a bad habit." Ariel's hand gripped his really tightly when she heard the voice and she tried to whisper but it came out very loud as she had no volume control. "Someone is behind us, mister." Paul started to make a slow turn while holding on to Ariel's hand so she would hopefully turn with him but slightly position her behind himself once they had made the 180-degree turn. He was successful in doing so as when he was finally face-to-face with the voice, Ariel was standing right behind him while trying to peek out from around his right thigh. Paul raised the hand that wasn't holding Ariel's as not to spook the man pointing a .38 snub nose at him. He was now face-to-face with a very tall man in pressed Wrangler jeans, a huge belt buckle, a white pressed button-down shirt, white Stetson hat, and a badge. Paul cracked a smile that must have been visible to the sheriff or whatever he was.

Seeing Paul crack a smile, the sheriff immediately holstered his .38. "Why would you put your gun away before you knew who I was or what I was about or worse, what I might be hiding in my ankle holster? This is bad police work, buddy." The tall man smiled as he slowly walked towards Paul and Ariel. "First off, I am not a policeman, I am a Texas Ranger. Second, you would have to be one helluva quick ankle draw to reach down and yank a pistol out from under your pant leg while holding that little princesses hand and by the way you are shielding her, you didn't seem to be itching to get into a gunfight. Third, your pant legs around your boots are too tight; you'd never be able to pull it off. Lastly, I've been watching you for an hour. If I were a policeman, I would say that is exceptional police work, but since I am a Texas Ranger, I was just doing my job." Paul smiled and lowered his hand "Can't argue with that. I guess I will dispense with the small talk and Ranger bravado and ask why is a well- pressed Texas Ranger on foot out here in the middle of the Texas Panhandle, and secondly, why have you been following me for an hour? You have the damn badge, why wait?" Ariel tugged at the back of his pants and reminded him in her overly loud whisper that he wasn't supposed to cuss and "damn" was cussing. He ignored the scolding and kept his eye on the tall man as he closed the distance between them. "Name's Jackson Johansson, people call me Jake for short." He extended his hand to Paul as he was saying it. He had a very deep raspy voice. There wasn't much of a Texas twang when he said it. Paul thought that he seemed very polished or educated, he couldn't quite place it, but he didn't fit the uniform with the boots and hat. And that belt buckle! My God it was the size of a medieval shield! "I am Paul, and this is Ariel". The Ranger let go of Paul's hand and bent down so he was almost eye-to-eye with Ariel. "Hi there, Ariel, you don't look like a mermaid, you look more like a princess." Ariel couldn't hide anymore. This tall man had tapped into her thought process in seconds. Paul thought, wow, he is good. The Ranger stuck out his huge hand to Ariel. She was a little confused as to what to do but intuitively she stuck out her hand and shook the Ranger's hand. Her hand disappeared in that huge paw the Ranger had but he was as gentle as a lamb with her.

"I didn't introduce myself because I needed to find out if you were actually friendly. After that tornado ripped through here, there has been some crazy screeching noise and I wasn't sure what your intentions were. If I startled you, I might get shot.

And because of your choice of apparel, there is a good chance you are armed, possibly illegally armed, and not willing to discuss the situation rationally with a man wearing a badge."

Paul gave the tall Ranger a complete look up and down and decided he could trust him. "If I could find my bike, I would be armed, and you are correct, it would be illegal." The Ranger let out a hard laugh that sent him backwards to the point where his cowboy hat slid forward on his forehead. "Nothing like honesty in a relationship. Since you presently don't seem to have your bike, then there is no law being broken, and for what it's worth, I wouldn't give a shit if you were packing. I'm in the same shape you are, on foot, and trying to figure out what to do next."

"How did you end up on foot?" Paul asked the tall Ranger. "I was driving towards Hereford, a town about an hour South of Amarillo. I needed to make a quick stop there on my way to San Antonio. Sounds very Western but I was investigating cattle thieves." He paused and cracked a smile and finished with, "Cattle rustlers and posse's, can't get much more Texas than that. All I needed to do was holler 'head 'em off at the pass' and it would have been perfect." Paul laughed at the joke in such a weird place to be, but he really did think it was funny and he was beginning to like the Ranger more and more. There was something very genuine about him, very confident, but he was also tough. No mistaking that.

"I saw the clouds change almost in an instant. I knew something was really weird when my ears popped like I was on an airplane. Didn't make any sense to me but I caught sight of the twister forming to the South of me and thought I had time to outrun it, but the more I looked in my rear-view mirror it seemed as though that damn thing was intentionally trying the chase me down. I was up over 100 MPH and it was still bearing down on me. I felt the back end of the car lift off the road as if someone had just grabbed the bumper and lifted it up. My wheels were spinning but I wasn't getting anywhere. Then, it dropped me back down just as quick as it had picked me up, but when my wheels caught the pavement again, the car lurched and spun out of control. It happened so fast; I actually thought I was going to get picked up with everything else that was swirling around me. What's really strange was, everything went into slow motion. I mean, I could see things spinning in the air as clear as day, which included people. I knew they were dead and I just figured it was my turn. I said my prayer to my Maker and prepared to meet Him. Hell, while I was asking the Almighty for forgiveness in a hurried way – I even caught a glimpse of a Harley. It looked like it was riding the outside of the tornado like a circus act but decided at the last minute to pierce the heart of that thing and it disappeared. Wouldn't happen to be yours, would it?" Paul looked around as if he were looking for the rest of his crew.

"It could have been for sure. I would hate to hear that my beloved .46 is scrap metal. Could have been one of my crew. I lost all my guys and all our bikes. I have no clue where they would have landed. Damn shame actually. Some of the best men on the planet got sucked away by that thing. I can only hope they survived." The tall Ranger gave him a look of sincerity and replied, "I hope they are all ok too. Did you say 46, as in 46 Knucklehead?" Paul straightened up as if he had just heard the bells on Santa's sleigh. "Yes! Do you know about the 46? Was that the bike you saw flying through the air?" "Absolutely not." Jake said with such confidence. "I grew up around bikes, that was no Knucklehead. The good Lord would never harm such an amazing ride." Paul began to like the Ranger even more.

It had never occurred to him that a Texas Ranger would be able to identify a 46 Knucklehead flying through the air. He was still skeptical, but it did give him a glimmer of hope. "Where did you get the little girl?" The Ranger took his Stetson off and wiped his forehead of sweat as he was saying it. "I found her in a cornfield ditch covered in hay and corn stalks. I think she landed there but the ditch might have saved her life. I told her I would help her find her daddy if she would stop crying. I'm not sure which is worse, her crying or her talking. She can talk the leaves off a tree." Jake looked over to where the little girl was sitting against a tree holding up a clover to the now very bright sun. "She isn't saying much right now, she seems distracted." "Give her time, she heats up like a microwave and then you start looking for her off switch." Paul looked North and then looked South. "North is Amarillo and you say it was hit pretty hard. South is Lubbock, but I don't feel like walking that far. I say we head to Amarillo and hope to run into some-one that can give us a ride. Stay on I-27 so we can be seen." Jake nodded his head in agreement.

As he was nodding his head, he spotted a flash a few yards away from where they were standing. Then they all heard the screech; distant for sure but just as creepy. Ariel jumped up from where she was leaning against the tree and made a bee-line for Paul. When she got to him, she sprang into his arms. It struck Paul as amusing that he actually expected her to do that and even more amusing, he didn't mind. Jake looked at Paul and Ariel as he said, "We need to head slightly Northeast so we can end up on 27. From there we will get picked up. We won't find anyone out here so let's get moving." With Ariel still firmly gripped in his arms, Paul took three steps toward Jake so that they were shoulder-to-shoulder. When the two were side-by-side they began walking North. Paul started speaking to Jake out of the side of his mouth in a very hushed and guarded tone as not to draw attention to what was now slowly following them. "Jake – I swear there is something or someone behind us about 20 yards." Jake kept his chin straight as if he hadn't heard what Paul had said but he had heard it. "Yeah, I saw it a few minutes ago. I couldn't tell what it is, but I clicked the safety off my .38 a little while back."

Chapter 14

JACK OPENED HIS EYES when the storm passed. His skin was stinging from the pelting he had taken. He looked to his left and was relieved to see that everyone was still intact. The rest of the guys started to open their eyes and check their extremities to make sure they were all still intact. Still squinting a little, he looked to his right where the Boss had been just a few minutes ago and found nothing. He was no longer there. He felt a sense of panic raise up in his chest. He looked down the slope of the underpass and could see that there were a few motorcycles still standing, apparently not a scratch and still on the kickstand. He wished he could have seen how the storm went through the process of picking and choosing which bikes to take and destroy and which ones it decided to leave untouched by the violence that had once surrounded them. He started calling for the Boss, as did the rest of the crew, but there was no answer.

All of them slid down the slope of the underpass almost in unison. That had to have looked strange to the cars passing by. I-27 was covered in debris so the cars that were now slowly passing by were weaving in and around the stuff lying in road. Surprisingly, every car stopped and rolled down their windows and asked if they were ok or if they needed any help. These folks in the West Texas Panhandle were what everyone said they were, friendly as hell. Most folks won't roll up on a biker gang. They were all wearing their colors, but it didn't seem to bother these folks. Jack and the rest of the crew started to assemble again. There was a total of 12 bikes still completely intact. That was amazing. The others were either in a tangled heap in the field across the interstate or they were completely carried away.

The Boss's bike was missing and worse, so was the Boss. Without any argument from anyone, Jack assumed command of the group very quickly. Despite their appearances, it was a solid group of men. They all knew their places and they all knew their roles. They had respect for structure and they had respect for Jack. He was the longest surviving member of the group. He had seen leadership changes and never once thought he was overlooked or felt slighted because he was never named chapter president. The one pressing concern was that they needed to find the Boss and they needed to find the Boss's bike, Michele.

Michele had the saddlebags and without Michele, they were not in business. On the priority scale, it was more important to find the Boss's bike than it was to find the Boss. It was a business transaction that needed to happen and if he had learned anything from the Boss, never let emotions get in the way of business. It was a bad habit and in their line of work, he had seen it too often, and it could be fatal. He gathered everyone up for a quick pow- wow, asked each man to spread out, cover the fields both East and West, and look for the Boss and any bikes that might be salvageable. He asked them to give serious focus on the Boss's bike, Michele. That bike needed to be found.

Chapter 15

ANNEMARIE WAS POLISHED and lovely as Mark ever remembered. He was definitely going to keep his distance from her at this meeting. Damn that garlic breath. He was regretting it big-time at the moment. She strolled into the Oval Office with her shoulders square and her chin parallel to the ground. She had chosen her white Naval Officer's uniform for her meeting with the President and Mark thought she looked amazing. He thought if only they would let the ladies jazz it up with some better shoes, she would be even more stunning. Even with the drab white pumps she was still a 9. "Admiral, thank you for getting here so quickly. I cannot believe you rode in a Raptor dressed like that and managed to walk in here without a wrinkle." Jim laughed as he said it and moved toward her to shake her hand.

Before he could extend his hand, she went full salute on him, as was protocol. Jim always forgot that part of the job but returned the salute. After the formality of saluting the commander in chief was over, he shook her hand as he did with everyone. Jim had such a disarming manner with everyone who visited the Oval Office. He understood the magnitude of the job very well, but he also understood the impression the office had on visitors all by itself. He made sure that everyone, regardless of stature, who had the privilege of visiting the Oval Office left knowing that they were not only welcome, they were now an official part of history as each visitor is registered. "Sir, I was in fatigues, I changed when we landed at Andrews." Mark stepped towards Annemarie to offer his own less formal greeting when he felt the toe of his shoe dig into the carpet like a ski pointed directly South and lost his balance. He stumbled right into Annemarie, nearly knocking her into the Abraham Lincoln bust that was directly behind her. To her credit, she was sturdy enough to catch him with both arms before he sprawled completely out on the floor.

As embarrassing as the awkward tumble was, it was even more embarrassing that in the unintended emergency embrace the two had, Mark somehow ended up embracing Annemarie around her waist with his face in her stomach and his hand firmly on her ass. He couldn't get himself upright fast enough to remove his hand from her backside in what he considered to be adequate time. She helped him steady himself and when he was finally upright and standing just inches away from her face, she surprised him by giving him a slight kiss on the cheek. Now he was really embarrassed. He stuck out his hand to say hello and to offer gratitude for coming but all that came out was, "What was that for?" He figured his face was beet red when he spoke. He could see the President laughing hysterically behind him but for some reason he couldn't hear him. He could only hear Annemarie.

Annemarie smiled, rubbed his shoulder, and without missing a beat replied, "The last man to grab my ass like that was my late husband and he always expected a kiss to go with it. It must have been reflexive." Now the President was bent over laughing with tears streaming down his face. "Uh, Mark, buddy, are you ok? I haven't seen action like that in years. Good thing she is combat-ready or you might have had a nasty spill!" Mark shook his head and looked down at the floor like a boy who just wet his pants. "I am very sorry, ma'am, I somehow caught my shoe on the carpet. I never intended to greet you in such a way. I am normally not this clumsy." He stuck out his hand again and she took it this time.

He felt her hand in his and he knew she knew how he felt. He just knew that she had that woman radar thing that let them know when a guy is hopelessly in love with them and they now had all the power. "It's quite all right, Mr. Dresnek, it was a harmless accident that I quite enjoyed." She smiled as she said it and what really caught Mark's attention was the fact that she winked at him in such a way that the President could not see her wink. Oh my god! he thought, could she have just flirted with me? He decided the matters at hand were more pressing than his love life and decided he better help the President get things back on a more official path. He could revisit her wonk later for sure. And he would.

"Annemarie, we had some very disturbing weather patterns this morning that Mark here thinks are some sort of attack, perhaps man-made. We had 165 reported tornadoes across the United States at precisely the same time. Fortunately, most were harmless and petered out quickly." Jim caught himself when he said "petered out" and wondered to himself if that was the appropriate choice of words for a lady, but he figured she was a soldier and had heard far worse in the trenches. "Others were not quite so harmless; the Texas Panhandle got its teeth kicked in with Amarillo and Lubbock torn to hell. Pueblo and Boulder were beat up as bad as Lubbock and Amarillo and we are hearing that Helena, Montana took a direct hit too. The line of destruction stretches from San Antonio all the way up to Helena."

The President paused to let her think about it for a few minutes then asked the question, "Annemarie, do you think this could be an attack of some kind?" Without hesitation Annemarie replied, "No, Sir, I do not believe that anyone has developed the technology to alter the weather in such a destructive way." Mark stepped in and said, "I've seen those science experiments where a kid can create a volcano with some soda and can create a funnel cloud in a giant pickle jar…you're saying that can't be done on a larger scale?" Mark heard the words come out of his mouth and wished he had chosen something a little more professional sounding than a kid's science experiment and a pickle jar. She probably thinks I am a dumbass. He knew he had to quit worrying about what she thought of him if he wanted to serve the President as he was paid to do.

Truth be known, he would have worked for Jim for free. He loved him that much. "It is a very good thought process, Mr. Dresnek, and I have thought of that too. It is safe to say that nothing is impossible, but this line of storms runs directly from San Antonio to Helena, Montana. It has been looked at from every angle and it simply appears to be a straight line of storms that caused high and low pressures to collide, thus the tornadoes. We have had weather planes in the air since this began testing the atmospheric pressure from ten thousand feet to nearly sixty thousand feet and there is nothing out of the ordinary. Like I stated earlier, the storms originated in San Antonio, more specifically, just North of a small town called Garden Ridge. There was a slight little seismic anomaly this morning around 9:00 a.m. but it was gone as quick as it registered with NSA." "Has anyone checked it out, do we have people looking into it?" "Yes, Sir, we have one very trustworthy man in Amarillo that was headed there this morning, but we haven't heard from him yet." The President wrinkled his forehead as he always did when he was confused. "Why would we send someone from the Panhandle of Texas all the way to San Antonio to check out a seismic anomaly when we have a major NSA branch right there in San Antonio? Doesn't make a lick of sense to me, Annemarie." He got a kick out of his unintended rhyme. His Texas drawl always came back when you least expected it. "Sir, the request was more of a training exercise. We have a Texas Ranger in Amarillo that we are considering for a post that may need to fly under the radar, but he is a good man and we wanted to see how he handled the simplest of tasks. This one was so small that we felt like it was the right time to try and get him some contract work in. He has a solid reputation and we think he can do a lot more than just hunt down cattle rustlers in Texas." Annemarie paused to allow for questions from the President, but none came.

Jim looked at his chief of staff and asked, "What do you think, Mark?" Mark tilted his head quickly then set it straight. It was a nervous tick he had had since he was kid. He had always claimed that it was from ducking too many fastballs aimed at his head, but it was more hereditary than anything. His dad the doctor had the same tick. "I still think it was man- made. We have 165 tornadoes reported and it was a seismic anomaly? That just doesn't make any sense. Amarillo and Lubbock are a mess, no telling how many people have been injured or worse, killed." "I've already declared 2 counties in the Panhandle a Natural Disaster, so relief is already on the way.

I would like to get down there since it is my home state and survey the damage. I need to try and put people at ease."

Jim was about to say something when the secretary interrupted. "Mr. President, there is a call for the chairwoman from NORAD, they say it's urgent. Shall I put them through to your line or ask her to step out and take it?" "It's ok, Ellen, put it through." Annemarie walked over to the President's desk and picked up the receiver. She knew better than to allow the President to hear the conversation on speaker, not because she didn't trust him, but because she protected him. Based off her military service, she was supposed to be blind to politics but internally and secretively, she was in his corner 100%. He was the first President ever to nominate a woman as the CJCS. He really took a beating for it too. He never once waivered, throughout all the confirmation hearings he would simply send her a text telling her he was proud of her and to stay tough. She was loyal but the way he handled the pressure of her nomination told her that he was just as loyal. Pretty damn rare thing in DC.

She heard the voice on the other end; it was the head of NORAD in Colorado Springs. NORAD didn't normally provide weather reports but since she was in the President's office and had been summoned there in regards to freak tornadoes, she had asked them to bypass the national weather service and provide her with quality updates. The equipment they had at NORAD made the NWS look like a Lego set anyway.

The voice on the other end was quick in its delivery and she was off the phone in less than a minute. "Uh, Mr. President, there has been another line of tornadoes striking from San Antonio all the way to Lake Superior. It looks to be a straight line slightly Northeast. The hardest hit areas were Dallas, Texas, Kansas City, Missouri and Rapid City, Iowa. We have reports of roughly 163 tornadoes in this line. No reports of fatalities yet but considering it hit downtown Dallas and downtown Kansas City, there is probably more bad news coming." Mark knew there was more to this. He felt helpless and he was certain the President of the United States felt even more helpless. Here he had his chief of staff and head of the military and he was getting nothing but reports. All talk and no action. Typical for DC. "Somebody needs to get some answers pretty damn quick." You could hear the frustration in the President's voice.

Chapter 16

AFTER SHE HAD CLEANED her wounds and was satisfied that she was presentable, she grabbed the keys to the car and headed out the same way she had before she blew a hole in her elbow. She checked all the breakers in the garage to make sure they were all set then jumped in the car. She turned the key to her Lexus but there was nothing. "Shit! I can't believe this is happening now! After all I have been through today, the damn car won't start!" She banged her hand on the steering wheel out of frustration, but it wasn't loud enough to hear the tapping on the driver's side window.

She sat in silence for a moment thinking through what she should do. She wondered if she had any jumper cables and even if she did, what good would that do, there were no other cars in the garage to give her a jump. There was the neighbor next door, but he was old and widowed; seemed nice enough but she was certain he wanted to give her a jump too. No way she was asking him, he gave her the creeps, but not as much as the thing staring at her through her window. The eyes were clearly staring at her, but they were bulged as if they would pop out of its disfigured head. One side of its head was pulsating, almost transparent. The other side was somewhat normal with the exception of a case of acne or rosacea. The teeth were nearly perfect. Straight and as white as if they had been bleached. Its fingers were tapping on the windshield with more curiosity than intrusion but nonetheless; Renee gasped but did not scream.

The thing was half-person and half-something she was not familiar with. An alien was the only thing she could think of but that didn't seem quite right. What she knew was that when it made complete eye contact with her, something changed in its curiosity, it turned nasty. It smiled with its perfect teeth, only now the teeth had grown what looked to be like fangs. Renee was fumbling through her purse looking for the .45 she had just held in her hand. As she fumbled through her purse, she tried not to lose eye contact with this thing but had to look down for just a split second. When she looked back up, it was gone. SHIT! Now that she didn't know where it was, she gave her purse her full attention, long enough to extract the weapon.

She peered through her driver window looking down to see if it was crouching, waiting for her to open her door and gnaw her leg to a stump with those perfect teeth and fangs, but she could only see so far down. She heard something scamper on the roof of her car at about the same time something sharp pierced the roof, nearly striking her in the shoulder. She spun around away from the thing protruding from the roof of her car, but it disappeared as quickly as it appeared. Just then it returned with much more force, as if it was pissed that it missed. Fortunately, it missed again. She threw herself flat on the front seat facing up, she pulled the shiny .45 up to her chest and began to unload. She fired at the roof of her car in as many different places as she could. She had no idea where the thing was at, but she intended to hit it.

The noise inside the car was deafening and she knew it would be a while before her hearing would return, but she wasn't worried. She could hear the screech come from the roof of her car as the bullets pierced the skin of the creature, but she could see the silver dripping down the front windshield. She couldn't catch her breath. She had never been more scared in all her life. She had no idea what was on her roof and was in no hurry to find out. One of the things silver blood managed to drip on her elbow, the elbow that was burned by the electricity passing through it. And she immediately screamed.

The pain was excruciating. It felt like acid had been dripped on her elbow and she nearly passed out again. Luckily, she had nothing left to throw up or she what have chucked again. The pain left as soon as it came through. She looked down at her elbow and was astonished to see that the hole from the electricity exit was gone. There was no sign whatsoever that she had been injured. She wiggled her elbow and couldn't believe there was no more pain. What the hell? She decided it was time to slide out of the car and see what it was that was leaking silver shit all over the interior of her car.

Before she exited the car, she slid the magazine out of the .45 for a quick ammo check; she figured she had 6 rounds left after she pumped some hollow points into E.T. She was still shaking and was terrified at the thought of seeing that hideous thing again, but she couldn't stay in the car forever. She sat up, reached for the door handle, and gave the door a shove.

Chapter 17

PAUL AND JAKE TOOK A FEW more steps towards the clearing. With a continued whispered tone, Paul said, "Jake, I'm just gonna turn quickly to see if I can confront our follower. Keep the girl close to you." Jake turned around quickly in time to see a wild hog come charging out of the scrub. He thought perhaps it was the biggest hog he had ever seen and wasn't quite sure if his .38 could stop it, but he drew his .38 like something out of a Wild West gunfight and with one shot, hit the boar right between the eyes. After the hog was struck, it ran for just a few more steps and collapsed in a heap right at Jake's feet. By that time, Ariel was screaming with her high-pitched tone.

Paul pulled her close and forced her head down on his shoulder until he knew the boar was dead. "Holy shit, that is one damn big pig!" Paul said. "Good shootin', Tex!" He followed up with sort of a sarcastic tone. Jake bent down and pointed the .38 at the hog's head and pulled the trigger. "Just to be safe, sometimes they don't die so easily." Ariel stopped her ear- piercing screams and lifted her head. "Who is that?" she asked Paul. "Honey, that is what you call a Texas size hog, very dangerous. Good thing Jake is a quick draw crack shot or we would all be in trouble." "Not the piggie" she said, "Who is that over there?" Jake and Paul turned to look where she was pointing when they saw the thing staring back at them. Paul immediately tightened his grip on Ariel. Jake still had the .38 firmly in his grip. "Step towards me, man. Take it real slow." There was no response to Jake's request. It just stood there looking through them as if they weren't there. "Step towards me, man, raise your hands and step towards me. I am not gonna hurt you, just step towards me. You look hurt, let me help you." They could see its head was half normal, if you could call it that, and the other half was transparent. You could see it's brain inside its head as if it were exposed but there was a clear shell or something protecting it. There was enough distance between Jake and the thing that he felt like maybe it would be better if he didn't seem so threatening, so he lowered his. 38 to the side and tried to present calm to the situation.

The thing must have appreciated that because it also seemed to relax, for a second. Within that second, it flashed a smile that sent chills down all their backs and with incredible speed made its way directly towards Ariel and Paul. Jake quickly raised his gun again and pulled the trigger. The first shot must have missed because there was no reaction. The second shot struck the thing in the upper torso and it let out an awful screech. Jake fired a third shot that struck it in the neck as he was trying to aim for its head and missed low.

By this time, the thing turned towards Jake, changing its expression from aggression to fear as Jake fired the fourth shot directly into the clear portion of its head. He squeezed the trigger again but only heard a click. The gun was empty. Damn it, he thought. Two shots into the boar and 4 shots into this thing! The thing took a few more aggressive steps towards Jake but fell to one knee. It put its hand up the hole in its pierced head and brought it back down as if to inspect the blood. His hand came back into its view and it was covered in silver liquid. Jake just assumed this was blood. It looked back up at Jake, this time with very sad eyes as if it now realized what was about to happen. The thing looked at Jake and said with a distorted British-like accent, "I wasn't here for you." The thing looked around in such a peaceful way as if he was now comfortable where he was. "I've failed to collect but there will be others." It then slumped over into the fetal position on the ground and it expired. Paul and Jake had puzzled looks on their faces as they took a few steps toward the thing that was lying in a puddle of what looked like silver mercury. In a matter of seconds, it decomposed into nothing. As if it never existed.

Chapter 18

"ARIEL!" SHE SCREAMED at the top of her lungs. She ran in circles around the house, she was hysterical. She continued to scream the name of her baby girl in hopes that she would hear her. He jumped in the old Willys Jeep and drove all over the property. They had 200 acres to cover and he intended to cover every inch of it. His heart ached, and he fought back the tears. He was racked with guilt. If only he'd have been stronger. He couldn't pull the latch down on the storm door as the wind was wrenching it from his grip. She was in his right arm, his strong arm. Maybe if he had shifted her to the left arm he would have been strong enough to latch the cellar door as all three had hastily scrambled to escape the path of the tornado.

It had all happened so fast and he could only think to get back to the farmhouse where his wife and daughter were home sick with the flu. He made it in time to see them stumble and fall coming out the back-screen door, obviously headed for the storm cellar. He slammed the Jeep in park and ran to them. He grabbed Ariel with one hand and helped lift his wife from the ground. The roar was becoming deafening. He was screaming at them to move faster as they fought the wind and stinging debris that pelted them as they made their way to the cellar. He knew that no matter how loud he screamed, they could not hear him.

The sky turned a smoke gray color and the roar became louder. Out of the corner of his eye, he saw the barn roof lift away and knew they were out of time. He sprung the latch on the cellar door and shoved his wife through the tiny opening, and then he leaped to the bottom of the cellar with his daughter in his right arm. She was hanging on to his neck so tight that he felt like he might choke. He turned to grab the door and pull it in towards him. The force he was pulling against was incredible. He pulled down with all the strength that he had in his body, but it wasn't enough. The force of the wind was too much for his grip and the door was yanked from his grip and ripped from its hinges. The action created a vacuum inside the storm cellar and Ariel was sucked from his arms. His mind quickly assessed his options and he came to the conclusion that the only thing he could do was let the wind take him too, and maybe on the wing of a miracle, he would land somewhere near his daughter and they would both be safe. If not, he prayed that his and her deaths would be quick and painless. He felt himself levitate in the doorway for a minute and then he too was sucked from the cellar. She looked on from the far back corner of the cellar in horror as she saw her little angel get ripped from her husband's arms and then saw the look of horror on his face when he knew he had lost her. She made a motion towards the door, but it was too late to help. She saw her husband hover in the doorway as if he was some magician and in an instant, he was gone. The wind stopped, and in her mind, so did her world. What seemed like only seconds ago, she was lying in bed with her daughter beside her watching Dora the Explorer re-runs when the TV let out its emergency beeps and began reporting the tornado warning that urged persons in Randall and Potter Counties to take shelter immediately. She had been through this drill before and it never seemed to be as serious as the reports, but she had decided to get up, find Ariel some shoes, and go downstairs just to be safe. She was in no hurry until she heard a window break and she knew right then that she may have waited too long.

She swooped little Ariel up in her arms and was downstairs in a flash. She hit the back-screen door so hard she lost her balance, sending her and Ariel sprawling across the back lawn. A blanket of relief came over her when she heard her husband's voice urging her to get up and felt his hand reach under her and help her get to her feet. She could see that he had already picked Ariel up when they made the sprint of a lifetime to the storm cellar. She felt his hands push her inside the cellar but not before she caught a glimpse of the roof coming off the barn. Thank God they had made it to shelter just in time, was the thought going through her mind as she turned to see her daughter and her husband being sucked out of the storm cellar opening. Somehow it seemed that the vision of her family being sucked up by a tornado was in slow motion. It almost seemed as though she might be able to slow it down enough to help save them, but that was not the case.

Once it was quiet again, she stepped out into the rain to see if she could begin to find the pieces of her life that had been violently ripped away from her only moments ago. She screamed for Ariel and she screamed for her husband but there was no return reply. She frantically circled the house and was beginning to widen her search pattern when she heard her husband's voice. She looked towards the sound and saw him walking towards her. She ran to him as fast as she could and embraced him like she had never embraced him before. She could see that he was bleeding from his forehead, neck, and shoulder, and he was severely limping. She sobbed as she screamed Ariel's name.

He had landed about 200 yards from the house in the North cornfield but somehow had managed to land softly enough to survive. He assumed the cuts came from being mixed into a violent tornado washing machine with metal, wood, and God knows what else and spit it out with a vengeance. Beaten up badly and possibly a broken leg, he was alive and was now determined to find his little princess. In his mind, he had to; he was racked with guilt for having let her slip from his arms to the beast that consumed them both. Luckily, the old Willys was still where he had parked it in the barn. The barn roof was gone but the Willys was still there. He figured he could slowly drive along the irrigation ditches, but he had to be certain he didn't accidentally run over her for she could be under a pile of debris. He knew in his heart he was going to find her, and he knew in his heart he was going to find her alive.

Chapter 19

SHE SLOWLY OPENED THE side door of the car. She kept the .45 in front of her so if that thing did jump at her, it would meet the business end of it first. She glanced at the front windshield; the silver stuff was still rolling down the windshield. It was eerily quiet when she finally freed herself from the car and stood upright. She could see the thing lying on the roof of her car as it leaked silver acid all over the place. Its head was turned away from her, so she couldn't see that its eyes were open and looking at her through the reflection caused by a bottle of Great Value water sitting on a garage storage shelf. She slowly sidestepped to the front of the car so that she could circle around this thing and perhaps get a look at its face again.

As she was making her move, it slowly turned from its side as if it was lazily rolling over in bed so that it could look directly at her. She panicked and raised the gun quickly, but when she fired, there was nothing but a click. JAMMED! I hate this shit, she screamed. She quickly rolled through all her options in her head and they were limited. She could run back into the house and find the other gun, she could stand here and rationally talk to this thing; perhaps even ask it if it "comes in peace".

That sounded stupid even in her own head and was beginning a slow curse at herself for being silly when it gently lifted its head and said in the clearest and almost child-like voice, "I failed in my collection but there will be others." With that it rolled back over as if it was positioning itself in bed again and expired. "Hey, you! You can't just barge into my garage, ruin my car with your acid leaking mercury shit, scare the piss out of me with those nasty ass teeth, say something like that and then just die! Wake up you piece of shit! What the hell do you mean?!" She quickly moved to the side of the car where the thing had rolled to so she could be face-to-face with it.

When she was standing directly in front of the thing, its eyes were closed and what looked to be like a tongue was hanging out of its mouth just like a deer after it has been mortally wounded. She took the barrel of the .45 and nudged E.T. just to make sure it wasn't playing dead but based on the rate of decomposition that was now happening before her eyes and the horrid smell, she knew that E.T. was dead. She decided that she better call 911 and get some help before this thing completely decomposed and nobody would believe that she had a close encounter with the third kind. She grabbed the phone from the hall entry table and dialed 911.

The phone was tightly gripped in her hand as she listened to each ring. She thought it was odd that it was ringing so many times...aren't they required to answer on the first ring? Geez, what if I was being murdered! Just as she was convincing herself that she had dialed the wrong number, a voice came on the phone. Chills went down her spine when she heard the voice on the other end say, "Hello, Renee – 911 cannot help you. You are on your own – you must fight harder or you will be collected." Then there was nothing but a dial tone. She dropped the phone to the floor as the tears began to well up in her eyes.

Chapter 20

"MR. PRESIDENT I SENSE and understand your frustration at the moment. The most recent tornadoes have apparently been just that, tornadoes. There have been no reports of fatalities; only small injuries, cuts and bruises, flying glass, that kind of stuff. There are some people missing in the Panhandle area that cause some concern." The President shot a look at Annemarie that seemed to infer that she was nuts. "All these tornadoes that run from the South to the North and nobody got hurt, that's what you are telling me?" "It seems that way, Sir." "And why are the missing people in the Panhandle a concern to the security of our nation? It would seem like we need to help the state of Texas find them with whatever help they need, but it is a local problem, not a national one."

Annemarie looked around the Oval Office for a moment. She had been in the Oval Office before, several times in fact, but she could never get over the power the room had on her. She reflected on the great decisions that had been made, the significance of history that passed through these walls. She was a patriot for sure and the office of the President of the United States was a place that often left her speechless. "Annemarie! Stop acting like a damn tourist and tell me what's on your mind!" The President always had a way of bringing her back to Earth. Mark stood over by the bust of Dr. Martin Luther King Jr. watching the conversation in his own speechless way.

He was speechless because he was completely enamored with Annemarie. He daydreamed for a second about how it would feel to take her in his arms and kiss her. No peck on the lips either, a full-on Turner Classic Movie kiss! "Sir, there was a motorcycle club that we believe was transporting a mutated version of the small pox virus." "Say that again, Annemarie, I am not sure I was paying that close of attention – it sounded to me like you said that a motorcycle gang was carrying the small pox. Did I hear that correctly?" "No, Sir, that is not what I said, I said that there was a motorcycle club that was carrying a mutated version of the small pox." President Stafford set his drink on the desk and walked towards where Mark was standing. "Mark, I am so relieved. You see, the head of my military just told me that Hells Angels was gallivanting around the country with a deadly disease stashed away in their tailpipes. I'm relieved, you see, because our original contract for the transport of deadly diseases was made with the local Troupe 103 of the Boy Fucking Scouts. I knew that contract had run out with them, but I had no idea we had taken extreme security measures of contracting a motorcycle club to fill the void left behind by the fucking Boy Scouts! Are you relieved too, Mark?"

The President's voice thundered across the room where it reached his intended target. He now turned and began his march across the Oval Office toward Annemarie. He didn't notice that his best friend was only a few paces behind him. There was no way that Mark was going to let Jim get anywhere near Annemarie. Although it occurred to him that Annemarie was combat tested and was a Navy Seal. She would have no problem neutralizing any man in any confrontation, but she was still a lady to him, and he was still pro-chivalry in every sense of the word.

Annemarie never even flinched and never would have. She was loyal to the President and Mark knew that even if his best friend completely lost his mind for a second, he would never get physical with anyone, man or woman. He just wasn't the type. The President stopped nose-to-nose with Annemarie and for a brief moment Mark wished he could trade places with Jim. He would love to be that close to her. "You want to tell me what in the hell a mutated version of the small pox IS and why in the hell the Sons of Anarchy are merrily riding along the fucking highways of Texas with it?"

She started to speak but he wasn't finished. "The small pox was eradicated off the Earth many years ago, Annemarie, and now you tell me it might be back in a mutated form?" "Sir, you are correct, the disease was eradicated with the last known case in Somalia in 1977. Atlanta has the original virus stored, however, we know through our research that certain Middle Eastern scientists experimented with the disease in order to make it less curable and deadlier. We also know through documents obtained during our war with Iraq that they experimented by injecting newborns without the families' knowledge in order to see how long and how far the disease could progress through natural human interaction with the primary means of first transmittal being breast feeding." "My God, that's insane! Evil!" Mark blurted this out without thinking. "Sir, we believe they perfected the mutation through animal incubation and fully intended to unleash it on their enemies through aerosol canisters, air dropped or perhaps timed release, on public transit. Either way, Atlanta had the mutated version under lock and key, but a rogue lab tech secured a strand through isolation and sold it to the highest bidder."

Mark could no longer hold back and was no longer consumed with Annemarie's beauty. "Why in the hell doesn't the President know about this already?" She turned to look at Mark but was cut off by the President. "Annemarie, I know about it now, which means that it is my problem and I better damn well clean it up. Which means it is also your problem and YOU, dammit, are my mop! Now tell me how the highest bidder was a damn biker bunch!" She shook her head and let out a sigh. "Sir, the biker group is merely the transport. I am pretty sure they don't know what they are carrying. If they did, they are braver than most. We had them intercepted but lost communication with them because of the tornado."

"But you said you sent one damn agent from Lubbock after them! That doesn't make any sense! Why the hell didn't you call out the National Guard!" It wasn't a question; it was the President releasing his frustration. "Sir, I understand that that would be the first and most natural reaction. We did not intend to frighten the public by sending in twenty thousand troops dressed in hazmat suits to apprehend a bunch of guys on motorcycles. We believed that would have set off a panic that we might not be able to contain properly. The agent selected volunteered for the job and knew the risks. He intended on pulling the group over and being frank with their lead guy. We believed strongly that after the lead guy was armed with the proper information in regards to his cargo, he would gladly relinquish its contents to the Ranger and perhaps be on his way." "So, what if the bikers had been exposed and were now carriers. Those guys would infect all of Texas in few days!" "Sir, this is why you did not know of the operation. We planned to neutralize them at mile marker 144." Mark was shaking his head in disbelief, as was the President. "What do you mean neutralize, Annemarie?" Mark knew the answer, but he needed to hear it out loud. "Don't answer that, Annemarie." Jim was back in control and was speaking in very firm but clear and rationale tones. "Who was the buyer and where was it going?" "Sir, we believe the buyer was a Jihadist group posing as cocaine dealers from Egypt. We believe that the bikers believe they are running drugs, which is generally their normal occupation. We also believe that they were to meet up in Los Angeles where it would be placed on an Indian cargo ship where it would eventually reach Pakistan." "Jesus Christ, what the hell does this have to do with the tornado in West Texas?" "Sir, the leader of the motorcycle club is missing, he was blown away from the group by a tornado, and we are also missing the Ranger that was prepared to make contact. His truck was caught in the tornado and blown away. We found his truck but no sign of him or the group leader." "Let me guess, the group leader had the virus?" "Some of it, Sir. We have made contact with the second in command, he had some of it. What he didn't have was with the leader and apparently the rest was in his saddlebags. We can't find the bike. We are looking for a vintage 46 Knucklehead that was blown away in the storm. The President realized what she was about to say and mumbled "fuck me..." under his breath.

Chapter 21

JACK WAS ABOUT TO JOIN the rest of the group looking for the Boss and his bike when several black Lincoln Navigators rolled up. There were no longer cars passing by. It appeared to Jack that traffic had been diverted or completely stopped in both directions of I-40. He figured it was to allow clean-up crews to begin their work, after all, the tornado had dug up huge chunks of I-40 pavement and strewn it all over West Texas. Several men from each Navigator jumped from the vehicles. He assumed they were men, they were all dressed in funky black rubber looking suits. He couldn't see their faces either. Each of them was wearing a mask but none had air tanks. Weird get-up for the hot Texas sun, he thought.

Something seemed odd about their movements. They moved with a purpose. They weren't there to clean up the highway. He could tell by the look of them that he and his boys might be in some kind of trouble. Maybe they knew about the drugs? The first man approached Jack, he was shorter than all the rest of the men but he was much stockier. "Are you in charge of these gentlemen?" "At the moment I am. We are missing one man, and who the fuck are you?" was the last thing he remembered saying. One by one the men in the goofy black scuba suits rounded up the bikers and tranquilized them with a drug called Etrophine. It was a quiet whooshing sound and they each pumped the treacherous chemical into each unsuspecting biker.

The agents were coordinated and very effective in their movements. Etrophine worked very fast, paralyzing its target within seconds, yet not so harsh that it would stop them from breathing. The targets would wake up after a few hours feeling very confused but very rested. The tranquilizer worked in seconds as it sped through the bloodstream to the brain where it told the brain to go to sleep. This allowed the agents to collect the targets, zip them into breathable containment bags, and clear out of the area in less than 10 minutes. They were extraordinarily efficient. 10 minutes after their arrival on the scene it was if they never existed.

The agents loaded each bag in a controlled transport and had the bikes and their contents loaded on semi-trucks emblazoned with 4 Sons Moving Company on the sides. Even the trucks were quiet...whispering models of efficiency as they quietly rolled East on I-40 with their incapacitated cargo. The leader of the group of scuba men sat in the lead Navigator. It was the first transport behind the non-descript bus that now was occupied by a bunch of comatose bikers that may or may not be dead in a few hours. He pulled his phone out of his jacket pocket and hit one number. "Yes, ma'am, all of the targets but one has been neutralized. We cannot locate the leader. Yes, ma'am, he has one of the packs we are looking for. Yes, ma'am, we left two men on the ground and they will continue the search. Yes, ma'am, unless we encounter some kind of traffic or any other unforeseen impediment, we will arrive at the secured base at twenty-one hundred hours. Yes, ma'am, copy that." He hung up his phone and slid it into his pocket.

He looked around the cab of the SUV as if to be checking to see who was listening. It was more habit than requirement. It was just him and the driver. "They will have someone from CDC meet us there. She won't be in a good mood. She thinks we should have been able to locate the other half of this shit. I hate reporting to a woman. They get testy over the dumbest shit." The driver nodded as if to agree but interjected. "Colonel, you really should let that attitude go before we meet up with her. Word has it that she can crack nuts better than any squirrel in the tree." They both laughed at the folksy humor of it. "We will find out if she is a ball buster like they say when we get to Los Alamos. Step on it, I don't want her to get there first."

Chapter 22

JAKE AND PAUL STOOD IN SHOCK looking at the place where that thing used to be. It was gone. It had completely decomposed into nothing. It didn't even leave an imprint in the dirt. It was as if it was never even there. Jake scanned the area around them to see if maybe there were other little half- brained creepy looking things around but saw none. Paul had such a grip on Ariel that she started to squirm. "Hold me tighter, poppy, it hurts." Paul tightened his grip on her but realized she had just referred to him as her daddy. He shook his head with confusion, looked at her closely, and started to remind her that he wasn't her daddy, but he realized she wasn't looking at him when she said it.

Jake was looking at Paul with the WTF look on his face. Jake shrugged his shoulders as he was dropping the speed loader out of the .38 and inserting the last rounds he had on his belt. Paul stared at her as she looked like she was looking far off in the distance. Paul put his free hand on Ariel's cheek. He slowly turned her face toward his as he was holding her closely. That thing must have scared her. He wasn't sure how much more of this kind of crap he could take, much less a beautiful little girl who has now seen more unexplainable crap in one day than she will probably ever see in her entire life. "Hey – little girl, look at me, look at me." He snapped his fingers in front of her face, but she still had this blank far away stare. Jake walked over to where the thing used to be to see if he could make heads or tails of what just happened. "That little girl's name is Ariel, man, can't you even bring yourself to call her by her name, or are you afraid of getting to know her; you might get attached? She is certainly attached to you." Paul just returned a look of confusion back to Jake and continued trying to get her to come back to Earth. "And what the hell did that thing say before it melted?" Jake wasn't necessarily asking the question to either Paul or Ariel, he was simply thinking out loud as he always did when he was confused about anything.

His colleagues in the office would often give him tons of crap for being so transparent but they admired his confidence in his understanding of his own lack of knowledge in certain categories. He was never afraid to ask questions and he was never afraid to speak his mind. "He said he wasn't here for you." Both Jake and Paul were a little startled at how clearly, she spoke the words. Ariel always had that little girl tone when she spoke but there was something very grown up about the way she said it. "Ariel, are you ok?" Paul snapped his fingers in front of her again. "Stop doing that, my daddy does that in church when I am not being still. He says I get ants in my pants when I am in church. I don't really like going to church, you have to be quiet and you can't play. You just have to sit there and listen to a man talk about grown up stuff. If I don't like church, does that mean that God doesn't like me? Does that mean that I am going to the bad place now? Is that why that thing was coming to get me? I don't want to go to the bad place, mister! I promise I will be good. I promise I won't get ants in my pants in church anymore! Please let me go home, mister. I want to see my daddy and mommy again!" Ariel was back to her rapid-fire questions and comments.

Paul thought that at least she was all right. She was yelling in his ear, which he didn't like, but at least she was all right. As her voice got louder she started crying. Paul felt her little arms tighten around his neck and then her sobbing became muffled as she buried her face into the side of his neck. Paul could feel his neck getting wet from her little tears. He was at a loss. He had no idea what to do for her. He put the hand that wasn't being used to cradle her in the center of her back and made sort of a patting motion. "Geez, man, she isn't a pet, she needs to feel loved at the moment. She needs to feel secure. Your little pat on the back ain't gonna cut it." Jake laughed as he was speaking his mind. "Well hell, you come hold her if you're so damn good at all this lovey dovey shit." "NO!" She screamed. "Please don't let me go, I promise I will be good, mister, I promise to keep the ants out of my pants, don't let me go!" "Hey," Paul said softly, "I'm not gonna let you go, just relax." He felt his arms loosen but tighten if that was possible.

He was holding her, but he no longer felt awkward, he no longer felt like he might accidently break her if he wasn't careful. When that feeling came over him, he could feel her relax in his arms. She whimpered just a little more but then fell asleep. "She doesn't want me, she wants you and it looks like she is quite happy being where she is at. You aren't as tough as you think you are, killer." Jake shook his head. "She is right though, that thing looked at me and said it wasn't here for me and it failed to collect. What the hell does that mean and what the hell was that? How does it just evaporate into nothing as if it doesn't exist anymore? There isn't even a wet spot on the ground where it dissolved!"

Jake was waving his arms around as if he was giving an animated lecture to an audience. "I've never seen anything like that in my life! I need some answers! I am stuck out here in the middle of nowhere without transportation and this creepy dude and a wild hog attack me all at the same time!" Paul had eased over to where Jake was holding his private lecture as not to wake up the now sleeping little girl that was in his arms. "Keep it down, man. I am just as freaked as you. If you think I've seen shit like that before, brother, you are sadly mistaken. That thing was definitely after something, but it was very clear he wasn't after you." "I know! That's what's freaking me out. Was it here for you or the little girl or maybe the damn hog?! I can't handle it when I can't get my mind around shit." "I get it, pal, but get your mind around this; that thing said he failed but there will be others. We need to get moving towards town. This shit is too weird for me. I want to start seeing some more people for Christ's sake. Better yet, we need to find Michele and let her take us to town." "Who is Michele, man?" "My bike, brother, my bike." Jake shook his head again. "Should have known you biker guys always have a name for your ride." "Not always, man." Paul snapped as if he was offended. "This one was special though." Paul began walking East as he was saying it. "I know a 46 Knucklehead. I won't argue with that." Paul noticed that Ariel was now asleep and breathing very slowly.

Chapter 23

SHE SAT THERE IN A FETAL BALL, sobbing like a child. "What the hell does that mean that I am on my own?" She screamed through her tears. "I don't understand what is happening! All I wanted to do was go to work and have a good day and I get shocked in my own house by my own faulty equipment, I am bleeding out my elbow where electricity decided to exit my body and now some hideous creature is trying to eat me and is now dead on top of my brand-new car! I do not deserve this shit!" As she was going through her rant and cursing the creature, she looked up at the top of the car and it was gone. She hadn't noticed that it dissolved into nothing just a second after it warned her that there would be others. She immediately got to her feet for fear that the thing was creeping around her garage again. She checked the gun and tried to unjam it. No luck.

She was very comfortable with guns but unjamming a gun scared her. She had a friend that tried to get his gun unjammed and perhaps was too comfortable and too careless and accidentally shot himself in the stomach trying to dislodge a jammed cartridge. Thankfully he lived but the bullet ripped through his spinal cord and he now shoots from a wheelchair. She figured once this was over she would take the gun into a professional and let them fix it. She wished that the Boss were here.

She was scared now, which was hard for her to do. She didn't scare easily and was unsure of what to do. She realized someone was calling her. She felt a little bout of relief, but it wasn't like the voice was close, it was more inside her head. They were clear, but they were far away. She decided she needed a smoke. She hadn't smoked in years but for some reason she really wanted a menthol. Back when she smoked, she smoked Kool's. She loved it. She only quit smoking because she never had time. Society had changed so much that you couldn't smoke anywhere. She hated stopping what she was doing to go find a place to smoke. She was just too busy to stop, walk outside, stand there, and smoke with other people who had the same issue. She thought she knew where a very old pack of cigarettes was hiding above the refrigerator. They had probably been up there ten years and were stale as ten-day old bread, but she didn't care, she wanted a drag and she wanted one right now. After all, she had earned it.

With the help of a small step stool, she reached above the refrigerator and sure enough, there it was, a vintage, unopened pack of Kool cigarettes. She tore the pull string of cellophane and ripped through the folded paper at the top just like she had never quit. She smacked the pack against the palm of her hand, again, just like she had never quit. She slid one nice cancer stick from its coffin and smelled it. In her mind, it was divine. Now all she needed was a light. She searched a few drawers for lighters and found one in her favorite junk drawer. She clicked the lighter a few times but couldn't get it to light. She cursed out loud at her inability to light a cig- arette. She tried to think of old matchbooks that she might have but drew a blank. She leaned against the kitchen counter because suddenly she felt light- headed, felt the need to vomit again, and that's the last thing she remembered.

Chapter 24

ANNEMARIE WAS ABOUT TO SPEAK again when the President's phone rang. He walked over to his desk while Annemarie and Mark stood staring at each other. Mark felt like he had been busted staring at her, so instead of turning away, he decided the best move was to continue his stare. He wanted to convey some sort of message to her that he was very serious and concerned about the events of her clean-up crew but knew it was not working. He continued his stare hoping she would turn away, but she did not; worse, she intensified her stare at him, which made him weak. In his mind, she was by far the most beautiful woman in the world. He knew his real emotions showed on his face. He also felt like a dope because the situation at hand was extremely serious and he was fixated on her beauty. He had to clear his mind of this love struck goofy stuff and try and help his friend, who happens to be the President of the United States, figure this mess out.

Jim listened intently to his trusty secretary of twenty years for a few minutes and then asked her to put him through. He held the phone on his shoulder while he waited and glanced at his watch. He looked over at the two people standing in his office and said, "You two get on a plane and go find that other bag. I don't want to see either of you back here in this office unless you are here to tell me the situation has been neutralized." The President turned away from them and looked out the window located behind his desk. "Ellen, when I am finished with the secretary, please get me the Secretary of Homeland Security. I also want to clear some time in my schedule this evening to visit with the Prime Minister of Pakistan, it's time that prick learned which side of the bread is buttered." Mark and Annemarie were both stunned at the tone the President used. His personality was much more reserved. He was a soft-spoken collaborator. He loved to build consensus and took pride in his alliances on both sides of the aisle.

The way he addressed them was completely out of character, but both knew that they served at his discretion and began making their move toward the Oval Office door. "I mean it, Mark – do not fail me on this." Mark nodded and walked out the door. Chivalry had left him momentarily and he walked out in front of Annemarie. His head was cloudy and full of questions, but he realized his mistake in not allowing the lady to exit the room first. He turned to Annemarie to apologize when he caught a glimpse of Ellen. She was crying. Not sobbing, but you could clearly see the tears rolling down her lovely soft cheeks. Annemarie spoke before she could apologize for his rude behavior. "There is obviously more to the story and the President is feeling the strain." She pulled her phone from her pocket, found the contact she was looking for, and pressed the screen to dial them. Mark started to speak but she held up her index finger in that motion that said, be quiet kid, I am working here. Mark half-way resented it but then found himself looking at her in the way he wished he wouldn't, that stupid thunderstruck look that showed every weakness he had. "John -I need transport to Amarillo, Texas; indiscreet, but fast. Yeah – no insignia, not even a tail number. It needs to be cleared so let Langley and Homeland know. I want someone from CDC who knows what they are doing on that plane when I get on it and they need to be willing to get their hands dirty. Yes, your team will be fine. You still have Wally as your second, right? Perfect, he is a good man. No, I don't want you on the plane. I want you to park yourself at the Pentagon so I have a point of contact I trust. Yes, all secured lines, SAT phone only for when we arrive. I am not really sure, John, and I mean that. I am on direct orders from the commander. Oh, scrounge up some fatigues. Hang on, John." She put the phone to her chest and looked Mark up and down.

She put the phone back up to her ear. "32 waist, 33-length, medium tee, and a large jacket. He will need a lid and size 10 boots. Yes, temporary authorization." She thought about it for a second and said, "Navy, Second Lieutenant. Make the name on the chest Holmes, dog tags John C. Thank you, John. "She tapped the screen and shoved the phone back in her pocket. Mark was amazed at her accuracy in measuring him but was not sure why he even needed a uniform. He was about to ask when apparently, she was reading his thoughts. "My dad owned a men's clothing store in the old downtown square. Did a lot of business and was good with customers, he could size up a man very quickly. He told me that he spent all his time sizing up the outside of a man so I could go to school and learn to size up the inside of a man. He made a good living, then Walmart came to town and ruined Mayberry for everyone. When I graduated from Annapolis, he was the sharpest-dressed custodian at the high school. What he didn't realize was that I didn't need to go to school to learn how to size up the inside of man. He taught me that every day of his life. He was a hard-working remarkable man. He passed away in 2008. Anyway, was I right on the sizes?"

She smiled her crooked smile when she said it. "Uh, you might be too short on the inseam, I am 6-foot." She tilted her head back and laughed. "Horse shit, Lt. Holmes. If you're a hair over 5'10" I am Angelina Jolie!" She laughed even harder when she said that. "Besides, inseam doesn't mean squat, they tuck into your boots. I will show you how when we get on the plane." "Why did you pick that name so quickly? Is he an ex-lover or something?" Annemarie stopped laughing and looked at Mark with the most quizzical look. "You really don't know, do you?" He shook his head to affirm that he did not know. "I will explain after we secure the saddlebags in Amarillo, and besides, I might want to find out for myself." Mark was totally confused. "You've certainly lived a sheltered life, Mark. We have a plane waiting at Andrews we need to get to."

Chapter 25

HE DROVE THE WILLYS AS SLOW as its gears would roll. He scanned the fields close and far as he prayed for a movement, a flicker, anything that could give him hope. He kept the Jeep at the lowest idle he could without stalling it so he could hear her if she cried out. He screamed her name over and over until his throat raged with pain. He would never stop, even if all he had left was a whisper. He could hear his wife calling for the same angel he was looking for. He prayed that maybe she would be lucky enough to find her first, find her alive so that maybe she could forgive him for losing his grip, forgive him for not being strong enough to beat back the grip of that beast that took his Ariel. Maybe if she could forgive him, he could eventually forgive himself.

The Jeep stalled, not because he was idling too slow, it stalled because it ran out of gas. He placed his forehead on the top of the steering wheel and began to cry. He was the weakest man he knew. There was no excuse for losing his baby. It should have been him. He wished he were dead. These thoughts filled his head like floodwaters. He knew in his heart that if he didn't find his princess alive he would never be able to live with the guilt.

She continued her circular search pattern around the house, widening with each new circle. She sobbed in between her calls for her angel. She tried to focus on the slightest movements in trees, brush, and all the rubble that had been created by the beast that took her child and her husband. Thank God He saw fit to return her husband and she had no shame in feeling the greed in expecting God to give her back her child. Even in the midst of all this rubble, she moved with grace. She was beautiful in every way. Her father had warned her about the farm life and that she was not meant for it. He had warned her that the man she was in love with wasn't for her. He warned her that if she continued on the path she was on that she would be pregnant, broke, and full of regret. He never understood how he made her feel. How when he told her that he loved her and wanted to marry her, to take care of her and treat her like the princess she truly was, that she knew there was no other man for her. She had met her match and she loved him unconditionally. She knew he would be overcome with grief, as would she if they didn't find their princess.

Ariel was a gift from God. All the doctors at MD Anderson in Houston told her she would never be able to have children.

They told her that the chemo treatment she endured for her cancer had damaged her ability to have children. She battled Chondrosarcoma at the age of 20, a bone disease that she nearly succumbed to. She battled it the same year they were married and worst of all, married against her father's wishes. Her wedding was bittersweet. Her father so opposed the marriage that he refused to attend. The man she chose offered to walk away as not to come between her and her father. He cried openly when he suggested it, but she knew her father would eventually come around to him. She was hurt that her father would not walk her down the aisle, but she didn't care. She loved her soon- to- be husband. He was her soul mate. After Ariel, he was the most important person in her life. They had to find her; they had to be a family again. God was truly testing her faith.

Chapter 26

NORTHWEST HEALTH CARE was packed full of patients with cuts, broken bones, concussions and shock, all from the beast of a tornado that had just passed through. Luckily there were no fatalities, at least none reported. The emergency room was spilling out into the parking lot. Every staff member on duty was working as dutifully as they could to maintain the mass of people that needed attention. They quickly set up a triage area in the parking lot to evaluate the injuries and place them in an order of priority.

Priority 1 was potentially life threatening, unresponsive, or arterial bleeding. Priority 2 was open wounds but non-life threatening and broken bones. Priority 3 was bruises and sprains. Fortunately, there were no Priority 1's yet. Despite the outward chaos, everything was organized and running smoothly. The four doctors on staff were handling things very well. They were effectively using the RN, LPN's, and fortunately they had three interns that were of considerable help. Although it was organized, they were not prepared for the flood of injuries they were about to receive. The attending physician was paged to the ER and rolled his eyes as if he didn't already understand the gravity of the situation. He finished his last stitch to his patient's right butt cheek...a painful laceration caused by what the victim said was "barn roofing" that should have killed him. Instead of killing him, it just cut a hunk of flesh from the one spot on his body that could afford to lose the excess flesh. He headed down the hall to the ER entrance when he met chaos. It wasn't the same chaos as before, this was different. It seemed more frantic and the panic among the staff was quite clear. Apparently, Borger, Pampa, Canyon, and Hereford sent their injured to Amarillo as they had reached capacity hours ago. The attending took command quickly; the triage had to be expanded. He could see there were severe injuries, lots of them. He knew there were not enough beds at Northwest, so he started diverting traffic to the VA. It was unorthodox but necessary for the health and safety of all of the Panhandle, and it was the closest.

Chapter 27

THE WAVE OF PATIENTS CAME at a furious pace. The VA was not really an emergency facility; they did what they were supposed to do, they treated veterans. They did it very well. They had one of the highest service ratings in the VA system. One thing they didn't have was pediatrics. They were definitely not equipped to handle children, but they weren't about to back away from this challenge. The community needed them, and they were going to deliver. They dispensed with the normal entry procedures and simply started treating patients. They could handle anything thrown at them. They set up triage just like Northwest had but they had much more room inside to handle the flow.

The first few that were quickly triaged into first priority were burn and shock victims. They were very serious burns. One had burns over two-thirds of his body and was in excruciating pain. They gave him a slow morphine drip to calm him and moved him to the burn unit. The second burn victim was a woman who had burns on the left side of her body. The burns weren't severe, but she was not responding when she arrived and according to the paramedics, she had flat-lined in the ambulance on the way over. They would have taken her to their base at Northwest, but the VA was closer. They were scared to take any more chances with her.

The head of the burn unit was the highest-ranking physician on- site and she was a very capable doctor. The name on her badge said Dr. Michelle Hundlee. She was tall, slender, and deceptively beautiful. She served two tours in Iraq and one tour in Afghanistan. She was a skilled surgeon and tough as nails. She was head of the burn ward because she was good with the patients, and she understood their pain.

Her MASH unit had been hit by friendly fire and she had suffered terrible burns on her left leg. She spent months in rehab in the scrub bath, crying in pain, and looking down at her left leg that would never look good in shorts again. It seemed like a weird thing to think at the time, but she couldn't help it. The Army never admitted it, but she knew it. She also knew that when you were in the business of killing people, bad things happened. She didn't necessarily enjoy being in the Army, but they paid for medical school and she was paying back her debt. No matter how much she tried to detach herself from her patients and just be a doctor, she couldn't. The boys and girls came in missing limbs or badly burned; they would scream in pain and scream for their mothers. They were in a bad spot and it was her job to help them get out of it. She patched them up in remarkable ways and too often sent them back to the battlefield.

Throughout today's chaos, she took command, which she always did. Her staff joked with her that if she had stayed in she would have become a General. She was that type of leader. She gave directions quickly and accurately, sorting out which patients needed the most attention. She moved people quickly and they all responded well to her. She moved two men to the top of the line. Both had severe head injuries. One's face was so swollen she could barely tell if he was male or female. He was not responding and is eyes were swollen so badly that she had a difficult time reading his pupils. She checked his pulse, which was running like speeding train. She didn't think he would make it, but she sent him to head trauma STAT. She moved to the other man who was tall. He is very fit and quite attractive, she thought to herself.

He had no real apparent signs of injuries, but he was not responding to any stimulation. His blood pressure was dangerously low and before she could issue directions to get him to X-ray to scan for internal injuries, he crashed. With the help of the ER nurse, she began CPR. She had dealt with this in Afghanistan. They would bring boys in that looked perfectly healthy and two seconds later she was shooting them with adrenalin or pounding on their chests trying to give them one more shot at life. No matter how many times she did it, it got to her. She cried on the bad days and prayed for peace on the good days. She managed to win this tiny skirmish with God today as she stabilized him with her experience and her determination.

Once she had him stabilized, she sent him off to radiology to find what was busted on his inside. She prayed they could fix him before he crashed again. The rush of her own adrenaline she felt after temporarily saving that man's life heightened her senses. She looked around the ER where she saw the children on gurneys and her heart sank. Apparently, a school bus tried to outrun the storm and ended up becoming its main course. Children were every-where; they were lost, scared, and needed attention and a soft touch. She knew that was not her cup of tea, so she assigned the oncologist on duty the task. She was a sweet woman who had seen so much in her time and she had a mother's touch. The oncologist took the role of pediatric care and ran with it. There were at least twenty kids, but a quick glance told her that thankfully, most were just scared, however there was one child with very apparent head injuries and was unresponsive. Her pupils were fixed and dilated, and her BP was extremely low. She quickly decided she need to move out of the ER, so she moved this young girl to the head of the line and sent her to head trauma on a gurney.

The orderlies wheeled her to the elevator where she went to the third floor. There she was wheeled into a very large room with at least six beds. She was hooked up to IV's and a heart monitor and was breathing normally but very unresponsive. She would have to wait for the head trauma surgeon to examine her. He wouldn't make it to her room before her blood pressure crashed and she went into cardiac arrest.

Chapter 28

"LET ME SEE YOUR SALUTE, Lieutenant". The van was at top speed almost as soon as they closed the door. The driver knew the urgency. Annemarie was sitting directly across from Mark on the ride to Andrews. "What?" He was caught off-guard. He wasn't sure what she was talking about. "Your fatigues are in the seat beside you. Better put them on but first let me see your salute." Mark looked at the seat next to him and sure enough there was a pile of clothes there along with a hat and boots. "My salute, you mean like a soldier thing?" Annemarie shook her head in frustration. "We will be at Andrews in 10 minutes. When we step out of this van, you are Lt. John C. Holmes. You better have those fatigues on and you better know how to salute when we get there." She popped a crisp salute at him. "Like this." Mark returned it with the wrong hand and even on the wrong side for a salute; it was far too casual for her. "Wrong side, pretty boy, and you better tighten up and sharpen that elbow!" She reached over and gave him a very hard slap across the right side of his face. It caught him off-guard. He had never been hit by a woman, for that matter, he had never been hit by anyone. He couldn't remember ever being in a fight. He never really had any reason to be in one as best he could recollect. "Do it again like you mean it!" Mark may not have been a fighter, but he was a quick learner with a very high IQ. He popped off a salute with his right hand crisply against the corner of his right eyebrow that would have made John Wayne proud. He wasn't about to get hit again. "Damn, not only are you pretty, you just might have a little soldier in you!" She shot off that crooked smile that drove him crazy. "Put the damn fatigues on or I'll really start wailing away." "Right here?" "Yes, right here. When we step out of this van you better be a soldier. Chin out, chest out, walk with a purpose, and salute smartly." He grabbed the clothes and started undressing.

At first, he was uncomfortable changing in front of Annemarie, but she got a phone call that distracted her a little. As he was unbuckling is pants, he realized that today of all days, he was going commando. This was going to be very awkward. He had flashbacks of her slapping him in the face and decided he better let Johnny loose no matter what or he was going to get hit again. He yanked his slacks down with the speed of Flash Gordon and got his fatigues on in seconds. He never even looked up to see if she was watching but he could hear her talking so at least she was distracted. Just before they rolled through the security gates at Andrews, he buttoned his last button on his jacket and placed his hat firmly in position.

He took a quick glance down at the name on the chest and sure enough it said Holmes. "How in the world do they have a uniform made up for me so quickly?" She crossed her legs, leaned back in her seat and said, "Lt. Holmes, your job is not to ask when and why, yours is to do and die." She had no smile on her face when she said it. It made him feel very uneasy and suddenly didn't feel like talking. "When we step out of the van, there will be an MP usher to the plane; he will salute me, there will be no need for you to return the salute as he will not notice protocol. The only things he will notice are the stars on my shoulder. Should anyone else salute you when we are not walking together, you damn sure better return that salute you just shot me. When someone is walking towards you, you need to be quick with the reading of their body language. If it appears that they are not saluting you first, it means they outrank you. You fire off a sharp salute and move on. If you accidently salute someone you are not supposed to, no big deal. They will just walk away and lump you into their 'Dumbass Officer' conversations they have when they are getting drunk."

She could sense that he was worried and tried to relieve him with some compliments on how good he looked as Lt. Holmes, John C. "Relax, Mark, we will be fine, but I need you to do what I say. I realize you aren't military and technically since you are the President's best friend and Chief of Staff, I sort of work for you, but you are on my turf here. I will take care of you. And by the way, you certainly live up to the name on the uniform." She laughed a very sinister laugh. He simply didn't get why she was laughing and referring to his made up military name.

There were no mistakes in salutes by Mark or Annemarie to Brian Wallace, who everyone called "Wally". He was a soldier to the bone. He was thick everywhere. To Mark, he looked like a bull on two legs. He had no neck that he could see, his forearms were massive, and his chest resembled a whiskey barrel. The guy was serious in tone, addressed Annemarie as ma'am every other word, and delivered one of the best salutes Mark had ever seen. "Wally, this is Lt. John Holmes. He will be your responsibility today. You will need to make sure that he returns safely, you have no priority other than locating our missing package. Do you understand?" Wally stood straight with his Mount Rushmore chin stuck out and replied, "Yes, General. He will be in pristine condition upon our return, ma'am."

Mark was amazed at the way military people followed orders. He couldn't help but think that if people on his staff and the President's administrative staff would follow orders just like that, they could get a shit load more work done. Wally turned to Mark and saluted. "Sir, Sergeant Major Brian O. Wallace at your service. Follow my suggestions to the letter when I give them to you and you will return unharmed. Do we have a deal, Sir?" Annemarie was standing directly behind Wally, so he was unaware that Annemarie was nodding her head up and down to prompt Mark on the correct reply. She was also motioning for Mark to salute. "Yes, Sergeant. We have a deal." With that said, Mark saluted the robot soldier which allowed the sergeant to go about his duties of securing the cabin.

Just as things were clear between the three of them, a very young African American woman stepped onto the plane. Annemarie turned to her. "You must be Olivia Millben from CDC?" The young lady looked very unsure of herself but replied, "Yes, I am." "Good, I am General Annemarie Dobson, this is Lt. John Holmes, and this is Sgt. Major Brian Wallace, but everyone calls him Wally. Have you been briefed on why you are here?" The young lady pulled out a brown envelope and handed it to Annemarie. "This is what I have on the virus's potential: what we know about this strain that they have developed and the effects if not contained quickly. Ma'am, I am not military, I am a chemist, a very good one at that. I didn't volunteer for this little hunt and I would rather not go anywhere near that stuff. I am sorry I am so blunt, but I was told that you handle information well, so you need to know that if one vial of that stuff breaks and becomes airborne, the entire state of Texas will need to be repopulated. Whoever made up this strand is evil, and I am scared. You should also know that there is no developed counteragent." Annemarie opened the envelope and went over its contents quickly, then handed it to Mark.

He went through it much more slowly than Annemarie. "Olivia, thank you for your candor. I will expect that candor every step of the way. From the report I just read, the strain has a 24-hour incubation period in the host, then it works through the blood stream. Is that correct?" Without hesitation, Olivia said, "Ma'am, the 24 hours is a guestimate. No one has ever dealt with this strand. You are correct that it works through the blood stream, which is what makes it evil. The efficient way that our bodies pump blood allows it to attack every organ in the body in a matter of minutes. The host will feel fine and 10 minutes later they are bleeding out every orifice of their bodies and in more pain than they could ever imagine. It is a very cruel way to die. NO ONE should ever have to suffer like that." Mark thought about that for a minute. Seemed to him that the vial must still be intact or they would have already heard the news of some crazy deaths happening in West Texas. "We appreciate your concerns, Olivia, I share them. I am scared too but for the good of a nation, I need your help. We need your help." Olivia let out a big sigh as if she had resigned to her fate, but Mark really admired the body language. He could tell Olivia was a patriot, a scared one, but she was ready to die for her county if necessary.

That alone was impressive. A very attractive young woman who yesterday was probably planning her next date was now on a transport with the White House Chief of Staff and the Chairman of the Joint Chiefs of Staff. She had spunk. Mark loved spunk in people. Yep, he liked her very much.

Chapter 29

THE BOSS HAD ARIEL FIRMLY against his chest with her head on his shoulder. His arm was aching from holding her and worse, she was sweating all over him. He wasn't about to shift her to his other shoulder to give his aching arm a break; he couldn't risk waking her up and he was enjoying the peace and quiet. This little girl could talk the ears off a rabbit.

He and Jake were having their own conversation now, but it was in a very low whisper. It was clear that Jake didn't want to risk waking Ariel up either. "How long have you been a Ranger again?" Jake thought about it for a second and replied, "Long enough to know better than to get into this situation. I swear I will never doubt a weatherman again. He said the chances of tornado activity were extremely high this morning on CBS. Most of the time he was dead wrong. He always seemed to predict a 30% chance of rain. You know in Texas that is meant to keep people calm. The reality is, if you don't predict upwards of a 70% chance of rain, it probably ain't gonna happen." Paul, stopped for a second. "What would you do different instead had you known about the storm?" Jake stopped when Paul asked him the question but he was now a few feet in front of Paul so he turned his head back towards Paul so he could see him. "I wouldn't have agreed to take this trip, that's for sure. I have a storm cellar on my property that is awesome. It has its own fridge and a submerged and exhausted generator with a buried gravity-fed gas tank. It can power the TV, microwave, A/C, heater and stove! For Christ's sake I could stay down there until the zombie apocalypse is over if one ever happened! Hey! That's it, maybe that thing was a zombie! Maybe we are the only ones left alive in the world. Ever stop to think about that?!"

Jake was starting to become more animated with his words as his arms flailed away like a maniac. "Dude, you need to get a grip. We aren't the only people left on the planet, we just got blown further off-course than everyone else. We are damn lucky to be alive. We just need to keep walking and we will run into someone that can help us get to Amarillo. Now keep your voice down. She is not breathing right. Her breathing is real raspy. It sounds like one of my brother's kids, the one with asthma. That shit is nasty. He has to carry around this little puffer thing everywhere because when it hits him, he can't breathe. I hope that ain't her problem." You could see that Paul was nervous. He may be one of the baddest bikers on the planet but whether it was fair or not, this little girl was his responsibility until he could hand her over to someone who knew who she was. Besides, he had grown attached to her.

Somehow, she had cracked through his outer protective shell and made him feel very soft-hearted and above all, protective of her. Jake continued his chatter about his superman cave of a storm cellar. He was obviously proud of the fact that not only had he designed it, he had built it all by himself! He drew the plans up on paper; had the plumbing and electrical lines on his property marked so he wouldn't accidently sever a power line or bust a hole in some pipes. He was quite proud of the work he had done to prep for digging a storm cellar. After he was satisfied he had completed all the necessary planning, he rented the backhoe and began digging. It didn't take long; he wanted a 12x16 storm cellar that was 8 feet deep. He installed the drains, pump, exhaust, electricity and water lines, and then he brought in all the cinder block and mortar and applied the moisture seal to the floor and walls.

Paul was getting very tired of the chatter and could not have cared less if he installed marble floors and a crystal chandelier. "I get it, man, it's a nice storm cellar." Jake almost looked hurt that Paul was not enthralled in his story. "Sorry, when I am nervous or searching for answers I tend to talk too much." Paul rolled his eyes a little. "That's not exactly a good characteristic for a Ranger. Don't you need to listen more and talk less?"

They both walked in silence for quite a while and Ariel's breathing continued to become raspier with each passing hour. They came to a field that was littered with debris from the storm. There were chunks of metal, tires, shingles, boards, and Lord knows what else. The whole place looked like a very messy junkyard. Along the North edge of the field, Paul could clearly see a set of handlebars. He nearly dropped Ariel in the excitement. From this distance he couldn't be sure if it was Michele or not but his pace sure quickened. "Dude, you see that?!" Jake looked around but gave no response, only a confused look. "The North edge, by the fence! See it?" Jake tried but he was unsure of what he was supposed to be looking at. Then he spotted the flash of chrome. "I see it!" He seemed almost as excited as Paul. Maybe they could fire that thing up and ride to Amarillo instead of this Walking Dead shit. "It's a petty treacherous path from here to there. Why don't I go find a path and come back and get you and Ariel?" Paul was having none of it. "Bullshit, here you hold her, and I will go find a path. And if that turns out to be my 46, I will ride the damn thing back and pick you up!" Paul gently placed Ariel in Jake's arms, which to Paul, Jake looked even more uncomfortable holding a little girl than he did. "She won't break for Christ's sake; just hold her like you give a shit." "I do give a shit, I just don't know much about holding little kids." Paul was already walking towards the fencerow before he could hear Jake finish his sentence.

He stepped across jagged sheets of tin that had been ripped from barn roofs somewhere. There was even an axle from a semi- truck; 2x4's with nails sticking out of them. He definitely watched his step as he navigated the minefield of rubble created by the storm. The closer he got to the chrome sticking out of the rubble, the more his heart raced. It had to be her. As he was contemplating how he could dig his precious 46 out of the rubble and bring her back to life, a bolt of pain shot through his body like he had never felt before. A pain so intense it dropped him to one knee. He thought maybe he had been struck by lightning but there was not a cloud in the sky.

He was about to recover from the sudden jolt of pain when another jolt ripped through his body. This one sent him sprawling on the ground. He couldn't breathe and certainly couldn't speak. He felt like his tongue was swelling to the size of a watermelon. He tried to divert his air though his nose, but it wasn't helping. He managed to roll over onto his back where he thought he was seeing the sky for the last time. This must be it, he thought, this is what a heart attack feels like. I can't die right now, I have to see that little girl get back home, I have to see Renee again, I have to tell her that I love her. We have to get married and have our own little Ariel. His mind raced through everything that he wanted to do. When he could think of no more things that he must accomplish before he died, he felt a peace that he had never felt before. Just before he closed his eyes and accepted his fate, he heard the voice say, "I told you there would be others, we are ready to collect."

Chapter 30

SHE FELL TO HER KNEES AND CRIED. Why so much? Why was she being tested so much? She had devoted her life to serving God and taking care of her family. She had been given a miracle in her little Ariel only to have Him take her back? None of this made sense. She felt a hand on her shoulder and turned to see her husband standing above her. He had tears streaming down his face. "I can't find her, baby." He kneeled down beside her and held her as tightly to him as he could. She was unable to control her tears and sobbing. She hurt, and she felt she had no other way to let it out. Through her sobs she managed to choke out a request. "Can you check the phones to see if they are working? Maybe we can call the hospital to see if anyone has seen her." He gently kissed her on the top of her head as he was rising from being beside her. "I will but please come inside with me. I can't be alone anymore. I need you. I am not sure what to do. I am not sure how to handle this." Without saying a word, through her tears and sobs, she shook her head no and continued to cry on the porch. He took that as a sign that she was angry with him for losing his grip on their gift from God. He took it that she was angry and couldn't stand to be around him. He took it that she was angry and wanted nothing to do with him. He knew this was coming. When he was driving the Jeep around looking for any sign of his precious angel, he knew the blame would start soon and he knew there was no one else to blame but himself. He couldn't argue that he had lost their little girl. He couldn't argue that he wasn't man enough to hold her close and not let the storm have her. Her father was right, she could have done so much better and now they both had all the proof they needed. He didn't deserve to breathe another breath of air.

His wife couldn't help but think if maybe he was a little stronger, or a little faster, or maybe if he had fixed that hinge on the storm shelter door like she had told him months ago, that it would have closed much easier. He never listened to her. She could see things that needed to be done around the house, but he wasn't very handy. He was so good to her and Ariel, but he simply wasn't handy. He was a good farmer though. He understood how to grow things and can things so they always had food on the table, but he simply had no skill for woodwork or repairing things. She always had to fix whatever was broken. She was the handy one, not him. She loved him for what he was though, not what he wasn't.

He was an amazing father; hard-working, faithful, and she knew he loved her and only her. She couldn't believe she was even thinking bad thoughts about him. She rose from her knees and decided she needed to be with him the rest of the way. Through the good times and the bad, just like the preacher said when he married them. She walked through the front door where she saw her husband with the phone to his ear. She could hear him asking about patients that had been admitted because of the storm. He described their little angel right down to the shoes she was wearing. She could see him nodding his head and she could see the tears well up in his eyes.

He hung up the phone and slowly turned to look at her. "The lady at Northwest said they had patients because of the storm but no children that fit that description. She was adamant that she had been on duty since the storm began to reign down its fury on the Panhandle. She also sounded rushed, like she didn't really have time to talk to me. She actually hung up on me." He placed his hands over his face to hide the tears; she began to sob again but this time she embraced him. She held him so tight. He let his arms drape around her and the two stood and cried for what seemed like an hour. "This isn't bringing her back, we need to drive to the hospital and look for ourselves. We need to contact the sheriff's department and let them know who we are looking for. We need pictures of Ariel to show. We need some clothes that she has worn in case the sheriff's department has a canine tracker." He paused and placed his hand under her chin. "Baby, can you get those things for me, please?" She tried to smile through her internal pain and nodded that she could. She turned to head upstairs to retrieve Ariel's things. He turned and walked towards the dining room china hutch where he kept it loaded and safely out of Ariel's reach.

Chapter 31

THE ORDERLY HEARD THE MONITOR flat-line just as he was wheeling the gurney with the badly disfigured man into the poly-trauma ward. He slammed the button for code blue. The nurses came rushing in with a crash cart and immediately began the process of trying to save her life. They wasted no time and worked like a well-oiled machine. Since the head trauma surgeon had not arrived yet, the nurse made the call that the girl was too small for paddles and began CPR with very controlled and tiny chest compressions. You could feel the intensity in the room as they worked furiously to bring her back.

Each nurse was quietly doing his or her part in this battle for life while each prayed for help in his or her own way. "No way, man!" Everyone heard the orderly yelling. The heart monitor had flat-lined on the badly disfigured man. The noise of everyone working on the girl coupled with the new noise of another flat-line tone was probably more than he could stand. He had worked at the VA for nearly 20 years and had seen an awful lot in his time, but he had never been in a room when two people died at the same time. He had definitely never been in a room where a child died. He began screaming for help. He frantically looked at all the machines with their bells and whistles and beeps and wished that he knew how to use them.

He had never felt so helpless in all his life. It seemed like every available person was working on that little girl and if he didn't do something this man was going to die. He had taken a CPR class through the VA once but that was years ago. He remembered the dummy kind of creeped him out. They called her Annie and she had creepy eyes. At least he thought she had creepy eyes. They would all have to take their turns doing chest compressions on her and then they would have to do mouth-to- mouth.

That mouth-to-mouth thing really bothered him. He couldn't help but think at the time, what if it's a man? Could I actually put my lips on a man? He really didn't think he had the stomach for it. He couldn't believe that all these thoughts came rushing back into his head at a time when this man needed him, or at least somebody to help breathe life back into him. Just when he had made up his mind that he was going to straddle this man's chest and begin doing what he could do to help this man live, the head of trauma arrived and nearly knocked him to the floor trying to get to the man with the swollen face. The doctor made no apologies and took over quickly.

What was most amazing to the orderly from his ringside point of view was that while this doctor took over the man with the swollen face, he was carrying on a conversation with the nurse who was in charge of the girl. He was asking her a bunch of questions that the orderly didn't understand but every once in a while, he heard something about blood pressure and heart rate, but that was about it. He was impressed that the doctor could comprehend so much information about one patient while working on another. The doctor asked one of the nurses working on the girl to break off and help him, but they didn't hear him at first. The doctor was looking for something as he was manually pumping air into the man's lungs.

When the doctor realized he wasn't getting their attention, he yelled the name of one of the nurses. "Carlos! Break off and come here!" Carlos heard that loud and clear and quickly moved from one gurney to the next. The orderly watched with fascination as the group that was working on the little girl all shuffled to fill the gap now left by Carlos. He thought it looked like a group of puppies all eating around the same bowl; when one moves away, all the puppies shift their positions while they continue to eat. Before Carlos could join the doctor, the doctor ripped the man's garment open at the chest. The orderly couldn't help but think that he had severely underestimated the doctor's strength. That doctor sure didn't look like he was capable of ripping any-thing, much less a sturdy looking shirt. He thought maybe the shirt wasn't as sturdy as it looked; maybe it was old and easily torn.

Then it occurred to him that he could have been completely duped and this doctor was actually Clark Kent like. Maybe he was one of those comic books heroes. Maybe in the rush of having to quickly save this man's life he forgot where he was, or he simply didn't have time to change into his costume. Besides, there were no phone booths, and nobody used them anymore anyway. In fact, he couldn't remember the last time he even saw a pay phone. Oh, yes, he did, it came to him very clearly, it was in one of those Walmart stores. He had seen the out of order sign on it. Funny how clearly he was remembering the phone booth. He heard the doctor tell Carlos to charge up at which time Carlos grabbed the cart that looked like a mechanics toolbox. He had an internal laugh bubble up when he thought to himself that maybe the guy just needed a tune-up.

Carlos took two of the cables with handles and rubbed some gel on them. Once he had the lube ready, he handed them to the doctor. He gave the doctor the thumbs up sign and the doctor placed the handles on the man's chest. He pulled the trigger and things popped a little, but he must not have been happy with the result because he popped him again. This time the doctor seemed pleased and so did Carlos. Carlos told the doctor he had done a great job. The doctor replied with more orders for Carlos. He told him to start him on something with a drip and so many CC's. He turned his ringside seat gaze back to the little girl as he saw the doctor move in with them. Another dog at the bowl, he thought. They all shifted without any effort and nobody missed a beat.

The nurse in charge filled the doctor in on everything that had been done to this point and the doctor said something about adrenaline. He couldn't hear as well as he could when they were right next to him with the swollen-faced man. He saw this giant needle make an appearance and disappear just as quickly as it appeared. He hoped they didn't stick that girl with that needle; it would surely poke in one side and out the other. They all got very still for a second and all eyes were on the monitor the girl was hooked up to. It began slow beeps. It was loud then soft.

He didn't know what that meant but they all seemed to celebrate. Not the kind of high five WWF celebration, but more like when someone is speaking; you really have no idea what they said and when they finished you know you need to clap a little for them just out of courtesy for having the courage to speak in front of a group. He got the same celebration at his AA meetings. He was still fascinated with the way everyone moved. Both of their patients were alive because these people knew their way around the dog bowl. He laughed out loud, shook his head, and exited the room. His work was done, he thought.

Chapter 32

JAKE COULD SEE PAUL GO DOWN to one knee. At first, he thought that he was kneeling to inspect the bike, but after a few minutes, he realized that Paul was in trouble. He had Ariel in his arms and he couldn't move fast; he couldn't put her down for fear one of those wild hogs would charge her and he wouldn't be able to save her, or worse, one of those creepy things that disappeared right in front of them. He began to work his way through the field of debris, slowly and methodically. "Where is he going?" Ariel whispered very softly in Jake's ear. "He was going to find his motorcycle and he fell down, baby. We are going to make sure he is ok and maybe we can get his motorcycle and ride it back to town. Maybe even find your mommy and daddy."

She didn't respond right away so he thought maybe she was out again. "Not him, him." Jake was confused so he pulled her away from his chest a bit so he could see her face. "Who, baby? Who are you talking about?" She stared off in the distance and raised her little arm and pointed in the direction behind them. Jake nearly did a 360-degree turn but saw no one this time. "Go back to sleep, baby, we will be home soon." Her actions gave him the chills. He got the chills infrequently, usually when he was about to enter a building where he thought there might be trouble. He thought maybe someone was on the other side with a gun and would like nothing more than to give him another hole in the head.

He always felt like he was at his best in this condition. All his senses were aware, it was almost as if he could see through walls. He liked it and he hated it. He liked it because he knew it made him as sharp as a razor's edge and hated it because he was addicted to that feeling. He loved the high that it gave him. He knew that it could be his downfall if he wasn't careful. Some people bungee jumped, he liked to get into shootouts. He remembered the time he was a second-year cop in Lubbock.

He was called to a row of houses mainly occupied by college kids attending Texas Tech University. They had their parties and a fight every now and then, but it was harmless until Pearl Sauerbry showed up. She was a low-life drug dealer who liked to bring her goons and muscle her way into college parties. She would dump some cheap drugs out, get the kids high, then rob them of whatever they had. It was still relatively harmless until she decided to beat some kid from Odessa to death with a baseball bat. He caught up to them at their house on 81st street. He and his partner crashed the door and entered under a hail of bullets. His partner dropped in the first few seconds, which left him alone. The gunfight only lasted a few minutes, but it seemed to slow down for him; he saw every move every person in that house made in super slow motion.

It was almost as if he saw their movements before they even moved. He dropped six people that night and will never forget hearing his captain say that all of them had expired. He lost his partner that night, but he lost more than that. He lost his fear of dying. He snapped back into the moment and continued to navigate the path to Paul. When he reached him, he put Ariel down. He had to lay her down basically next to Paul because she was asleep again. He checked his pulse. They always did that part well on the TV. They would place their fingers on the necks and quickly ascertain if they were dead or alive.

He was never sure if he had his fingers in the right place. He moved his fingers all over Paul's neck and decided he didn't have a pulse. He checked his tongue and airway, seemed clear to him. He started chest compressions. Thank God they finally said mouth-to-mouth was not necessary anymore. He pumped his chest at the base of the breastbone where they had told him in his life saving classes as a rookie cop. Ariel remained "out of it" as Jake did what little he knew how to do to get life back into Paul. Paul's eyes popped open just like he had seen in one of those scary movies. It was quick, and they were wide open. It gave Jake a quick chill, but he continued to try and get Paul's heart to beat on its own. After a few minutes, Paul's eyes closed. Jake stopped the compressions when he realized Paul was breathing on his own.

Chapter 33

THE NON-DESCRIPT PLANE without even a tail number was lumbering down the runway. It was a Boeing C-17 Globemaster. From the moment Mark stepped on the plane, he was in awe of the deceptive size inside. He had been on Air Force One lots of times and that was certainly the height of luxury, but this plane was nowhere close. To him it seemed like it was stripped of its guts and all that was left was the inside of the shell. They were sitting near the pilot's cabin in oversized chairs with huge armrests.

It also seemed like way too big of a plane for just four people, not counting the pilots. He could see that Olivia was in awe of the same stuff he was. Annemarie and Sergeant Major Wallace seemed to be right at home. The two were having a very serious conversation that Mark couldn't quite hear and perhaps he didn't want to when Annemarie's phone rang. "You didn't find the lead biker or the second bag? Well are you looking for him? Ok, what time will you arrive? You damn sure better not have any impediments, Colonel. We will be there before you. Step on it and Colonel, you can cut the ma'am shit. It's beneath you to patronize me." She slid the phone back into the pocket just to the side of her thigh.

That was another thing that Mark couldn't get over, these fatigues had so many damn pockets you literally needed a map of where you put all your things. He was thinking about the pockets on her fatigues and wanting so badly to see her naked thigh. He was certain she was all woman under that rough demeanor. Now wasn't the time to be thinking such ridiculous boyish crap but he couldn't help it. Annemarie had him by the balls, and the heart, and he wasn't sure if she knew it. He wasn't sure he wanted her to know it. He was scared to death of commitment. Always had been. He had dated plenty of women, he just never found one that really tugged at him until he met the General.

Mark was well aware of the whispers about his potentially being gay throughout the entire campaign and the whispers even claimed that maybe even he and the President had a clandestine- style relationship. It was all bullshit of course but he could never figure out why it still mattered who someone slept with, man or woman. He had heard from the staffers after Jim had won the election that the rumors of him being gay may have wrangled some votes from the left, but he had also heard that the rumors had drained some votes from the right. Who knew? He really didn't care. He just knew that every time he was around Annemarie Dobson he had trouble formulating sentences and in the back of his head he could hear AC/DC pounding out the tune of "Thunderstruck". He had no idea what to do with these goofy emotions, but he knew he needed to focus on the task at hand. He would never let Jim down. Ever.

He was daydreaming in his huge chair when he heard the voice of Sergeant Major Brian Wallace as if it was off in a tunnel. "Lt., fasten your seat belt." Mark was trying to come back from La La Land and wasn't sure what he was hearing. "Lt., fasten your seat belt, the pilot says it's going to be a bumpy ride to New Mexico." Mark heard him that time and nodded. He wasn't sure if he was supposed to say anything "officer-like" back to the sergeant or even salute so he decided to go with what he was most comfortable with. "Thank you, Sergeant".

He fastened the belt around his waist as snug as he felt comfortable. "Lt., you should use the harness too. These big ass planes are terrible about dropping rapidly in turbulence. The pressure on your waist might tug at you more than you want, especially in all the wrong places." Sergeant Major Brian Wallace laughed when he said it. "How long have you been in the military, Sergeant Wallace?" Sergeant Wallace smiled because he loved talking about the Marines. "Marines, Sir,

I have been a Marine for 23 years now." "Why do you say it like that, isn't the Marines part of the military, Sergeant?" "Sir, without the Marines, the rest wouldn't matter. We do all the heavy lifting. Anytime there is something that needs broken, we break it. When there is someone that needs to visit God, we arrange the meeting. When the lines are fuzzy and gray, we add clarity and color." Mark had heard about Gung Ho before, but he had never met it face-to-face until now.

He wasn't sure what to say so he went simple again. "I see." "Sir, call me Wally, everyone does. How long have you been in the boat, Sir?" Mark panicked for a second and quickly did the calculations and replied, "10 years, Wally." The sergeant was about to say something when Annemarie walked up from behind them. She had been in the cockpit gathering the correct information on flight time and arrival. Even though the plane seemed to be handling the turbulence relatively well as far as Mark was concerned, he immediately began to calculate how he would "rescue" Annemarie should she fall victim to any angry turbulence. "We will arrive in New Mexico at eleven hundred. The cargo should arrive at the same time. The decontamination and containment team are already on-site. Once we are secure and have reached a final conclusion on outbreak and spread potential, we will evac." Mark raised his hand as if required to speak. "You don't have to raise your hand, Lieutenant." Mark turned a little red, he had shown is hand.

He was used to speaking to the President and knew better than to be such a wuss. "What about the second bag, has anyone located it or is that our mission too?" She seemed to search for the correct words. He was unsure if she was guarded in her response because Wally was there or she was guarded because she didn't want to tell him what was on her mind. "We will decide that after we have assessed the situation in Los Alamos." "We are going to Los Alamos? I thought that place closed a long time ago... something about seeping radiation through the cracks in the sidewalk and toilets that melt your ass if you stay too long." Wally cracked a smile at that one. "Then I suggest that if you need to go that bad when we get there, you should make it quick. I'd hate to see your ass get melted before our mission is complete." "So, it would be ok to melt my ass after the mission is complete?" Suddenly Mark was feeling his oats.

He was cracking jokes and making a hardened drill sergeant laugh. He thought he caught a smile out of Annemarie, but she quickly removed it. "That's the most secure place in the region. You'll be surprised how modern it is when we get there. You will also not be able to tell a single soul what you see there for as long as you live. Any loose lips later and you get a visit from one of Sergeant Major Wallace's hand-picked jarheads and no one will ever know what happened to you. Poof, vanished into thin air." Mark saw no hint of joking on her part and it unnerved him a bit and knocked him off his game a little. "General, Wally and I have become close friends on this trip, he wouldn't hurt me." He tried to smile when he said it, but he knew it was a lousy comeback and he kind of even knew what the retort would be. "Beggin' the Lieutenant's pardon, but if General Dobson gives me the order, you'll disappear before you even know you've disappeared." Annemarie cracked a smile at that one. "Now, Wally, Lt. Holmes is our guest here, let's not mistreat him just yet. I still have something I have to find out about Lt. John C. Holmes."

Chapter 34

"MR. PRESIDENT, I have the British Prime Minister on the line. She would like to fill you in on some details that I am certain you will want to hear. And Mr. President, she doesn't want to be on speakerphone, I am sending it to your desk now." Jim was so grateful to Ellen. She was the best admin and friend anyone could have. She had been with him for so many years and now she ultimately sat in one of the most powerful seats in the world. If you wanted to see the President you had to go through her first. She also had his ear. You would be in a terrible position if you made a bad impression on her. She could spot a phony a mile away.

Unfortunately, Washington DC was full of them. She never tired of working for Jim, at least not as far as he could see. He paid her well from his blind trust through a different name. There was no way she could live in DC on the salary the government paid her for being the lead administrative assistant to the President. Her husband was a decorated Viet Nam veteran, with three Purple Hearts, a Silver Star, and a Distinguished Service Cross. He was an Army Ranger and tough as nails. He rescued eight men under heavy enemy fire when their Huey was shot down during an extraction mission. He lived through all of that and had been recently killed in a head- on collision with a drunk driver. The President personally drove harsher penalties for drunk driving through the legislative process as a result of his death. Jim loved that woman like he loved his own mother and she protected him in the same way.

"Madam Prime Minister, how are you?" There was a small degree of small talk, but it was not Jim's strong point as a politician or even as a person. He was a very direct person and didn't really enjoy party chat or small talk. He also knew that the Prime Minister felt the same way as he watched her at meetings and could easily sense through reading her body language that she didn't handle small talk very well either. He liked her but politically they were on polar opposites of the idea scale. She was closer to Socialist and he was closer to Conservative. Both tried to campaign closer to the middle, but it was difficult to hide. "Mr. President, I am to understand that you have a chemical weapon traveling across your states that is bound for Pakistan. Would I be accurate in my knowledge?" Jim was caught off-guard by this bit of information she had just revealed to him. How the hell did she know that? "Madam, I assure you that we have that genie almost back in the bottle." "Jim, you and I both know that almost doesn't count in the chemical weapons business. Please do not forget that I am your ally in peace and war. Our political differences may be vast but both of us understand the responsibility of our offices and the burdens it presents when it comes to the safety and protection of our people. We are cut from the same genetic cloth, my good man. Please be more frank with me and I will return in kind." Jim looked around the office, trying to work through all of his thoughts and what had to be done. Sending his best friend with Annemarie was the most difficult decision he had ever made and he felt the nausea rise in his stomach and had to force it down.

He was trying to process his words before he delivered them. He felt like despite their political differences he could trust her, and she had stuck by him on some of his decisions to increase troops in Afghanistan and Iraq. She committed more troops of her own and never flinched when her party chastised her for it. "Yes, you are correct. We have it 50% contained as we believe we are in possession of half of the shipment. The other half appears to have been swallowed up and spit out by a freakishly large tornado somewhere over the Panhandle of Texas. We have a team on the ground now that will locate the other half and get it back to Atlanta. That is all the frankness I have to share with you at the moment." He breathed a bit of relief as it always felt better to have an ally in difficult situations. Somehow it relieved the weight of "crown" a little as Jim had always operated under the motto of "even on the most exalted throne, a King sits upon nothing more than his own arse." The quote was always in his desk somewhere. "Thank you, Mr. President. I appreciate the candor. Do you know how the virus was removed from your facility?" It came out as more of a comment than a question and Jim recognized that by the tone of the way she said it. She had more information, so he decided to share what he thought he could about its origin. "We believe a rogue lab tech in need of cash decided to pad his 401(k) considerably and removed the virus from the lab. Madam Prime Minister, if you have information that I should have, please feel free to share it." There was a pause on the phone. "Jim, that rogue lab tech is British, he was put there by us. He was one of our most trusted agents but apparently, he went rogue. The person you have in custody is merely a patsy to theft. The real agent set them up in case something like this happened. We have the rogue agent in our custody at the Embassy in New York. Luckily, we monitor the 'monitors' activity and were delinquent in realizing that he was communicating with Pakistani officials though a fraudulent Facebook account. Looking at it now, it should have been caught sooner but it was not. I am calling to ask what you would like me to do with the agent. I can turn him over to you for further interrogation. Please keep in mind that as long as he is on the embassy compound he is not subject to American laws and furthermore can be interrogated by any means I see fit. I am not as strictly bound by laws as you may be." "Dammit, Abby! Why the hell are you spying on us and especially at CDC? I have always shared information with you and there was no need for a British undercover agent working right under my nose. This makes no sense." Jim knew all countries spied on all other countries whenever and wherever they could. Hell, the US did it better than most but in this case, it seems the Brits had edged in a place where they had ringside seats.

He had to sound outraged at first, as he was sure she expected. Politics was a show. "Jim, I offer no apology for protecting the citizens of Great Britain, as I am sure you do not have the time to clarify the list I have of all the locations of your plants as I am prepared to do if you wish." Jim smiled at the comment because he knew she knew where some of his agents were operating in the UK but not all. She was a tough lady and he enjoyed this type of backroom brawling. "Not necessary, Abby." "Superb, now we can move along at a more jolly pace." She was well-educated, but she also knew how to take it down a notch. "We extracted him before you realized you had the wrong person in your custody. Now that we have the communication lines opened with complete disclosure, you have more freedom to discuss what you would like me to do with this agent while he is on British soil, or perhaps you would like to send someone to the embassy to visit with him yourself? You and your agents will be given the utmost courtesy and cooperation." Jim was glad she was on his team. He knew that he could send agents to yank the guys' fingernails out while he was inside the British Embassy, but had they caught up to him before the Brits, he would have had to read the guy his Miranda Rights and every civil rights lawyer under the sun would have been jockeying to position them in front of a camera screaming about civil rights and water-boarding.

Abby had somewhat admitted her mistake and had made it right by getting to the British Embassy before any of that happened. "Thank you, Madam, we will handle it from here. I appreciate your cooperation. You are a delightful ally in such trying times." Jim turned to Annemarie and Mark and sent them to West Texas with a stern warning of not failing and he asked Ellen to get the Director of Homeland Security. The Director of Homeland Security was not a politician so-to-speak. He was a rough and tumble cowboy from Wyoming who loved to scrap. He would handle this agent at the embassy and get all the information the President would ever need. Jim would deal with Pakistan later. Right now, he wanted the second vial of the virus.

Chapter 35

SHE OPENED HER EYES. It was extremely bright. She had trouble getting her eyelids to cooperate. She squinted but everything seemed so bright. She decided to close her eyes because it gave her a headache to keep trying. She tried to remember where she was but was drawing a blank. She did remember thinking of the Boss and how he made her feel special. She remembered picking out a dress and shoes and was going to send him a selfie while he was out on the road. She remembered the lights going out and she went to the garage to flip the breaker, but she was a real blank after that. Her chest felt like someone had hit her with a baseball bat. She couldn't even lift her head. It hurt to do so. She knew she wasn't in her own bed because the sheets weren't soft.

They were actually very scratchy, and she started to feel like she was going to vomit. Not because of the sheets but because she was dizzy. She remembered that part! She had vomited somewhere but she wasn't sure where. Where was it, in the garage, maybe it was in the kitchen? Holy crap, what if she hurled in her bedroom and forgot? Her bedroom was carpet. That would stink so bad. She tried to open her eyes again and this time it was a little easier but not much. Things were still very bright and very blurry, but she could hold her eyes open a little longer now than when she tried the first time. She remembered a screech, a really creepy one. What the hell was that? She heard a steady beeping noise but couldn't quite make it out. It was faint then loud. She turned her head ever so slightly but even that little effort was too much. She just put her head back where it was before and tried to focus on opening her eyes. It was no use, she felt so dizzy and so tired and what the hell had happened to her chest? Her mouth was dry as a bone and she desperately wanted some water. Oh, what she would give for some water.

She fought as hard as she could to open her eyes, but it was futile. She couldn't stand the light. "You got quite a jolt. Just rest easy and we will get you back on your feet." Huh? She thought she heard someone say something to her, but she wasn't sure. It was faint and muffled like she had her head under water. She tried to mouth the words, but she couldn't. Her mouth was too dry. As a matter of fact, she had something stuck in her mouth. What the hell was that? "You're intubated, honey, you have a tube in your throat to help you breathe. We were afraid the shock would close your throat and we were right. You really are a tough woman. You battled as hard as anyone I've ever seen. You can't speak right now; we just want you to rest. Just try and relax. I will be back in a few minutes to check on you and maybe the doctor will let us take that tube out of your throat." She definitely knew someone was talking to her, but she couldn't figure out what they were saying. She closed her eyes and drifted off to sleep. She was so tired.

Chapter 36

HE TOOK THE FARM ROAD that connected to I-25 that ran North and South through Amarillo. He didn't take the Willys Jeep, it wasn't street legal. He was in the mini-van that she drove. She was sitting in the passenger seat staring out the window. She could see the path of the tornado in some places. He had to remind her to buckle her seat belt three times. That annoying little "ding" kept going off letting them know that someone wasn't secured in the cabin. He hated those things. He felt like it was an invasion of his own right to choose. If he wanted to die in a head-on collision by being hurled through the front windshield, that was certainly his right to decide, not some politician that was always butting into other people's lives.

When she finally managed to buckle her seat belt, he worked up the courage to ask her the inevitable. "What if we don't find her? What if she isn't at the hospital?" She didn't answer him. He had fought back the tears so much in the last three hours that he was drained. He had nothing left in the emotional tank. He felt the gun digging into his back where he had concealed it from his beautiful bride. He had seen the devastation first-hand. He had felt the power of that beast of a tornado pry his grip on his beautiful little girl as if he had baby fingers. He felt like such a failure. He was beginning to feel the weight of his predicament and to him it was obvious that there was only one logical way to handle it. They jumped on to Interstate 25 for a few miles until it intersected with I-40. It was the only way to get to Northwest Medical. When he arrived, he was prepared to check every room if he had to. He had envisioned smashing the doors open to the operating room if he had to. He was going to check everything before he went through with his solution. The parking lot to Northwest was packed full, as he had imagined. He parked the van in a dirt parking lot across the street where other cars had begun to create a makeshift parking lot.

When he put the car in park and turned the ignition off, she made no movement. She continued to stare out the window. He didn't say anything but opened his door, got out, walked around to her side, and opened her door for her like he used to do when they were dating. Somehow as they became more settled as a couple, he stopped doing those cute little acts of chivalry that he used to be so proud of. He stuck out his hand to help her, but she refused it. She slid her legs sideways and stepped out of the car. She gavehim a look, but her eyes were lifeless. He thought they had turned black, but he was sure he was imagining things. She didn't pick up the clothes that they had brought with them. He thought about grabbing them, but he would wait until they got to the police station. Maybe they would come in handy there. He wasn't even sure if they, or at least he, would make it that far.

The entry was as chaotic as he thought it would be. There were people everywhere. He went to the admissions desk and waited in line. He started asking anyone who looked official if they had seen his little girl. He was holding up a picture to everyone who passed by. He could hear the admissions lady telling one of the people in front of him that they would have to wait, and things were not normal. She stood as stoic as ever, she wasn't saying anything to him or to anyone passing by. She just stood in her spot. Every now and then he could see a tear run down her cheek but other than that, she was without emotion. "Ma'am, I am looking for my daughter." He slid her picture across the check- in counter to her. The admissions nurse didn't look at the picture and continued to scribble on a piece of paper. "Ma'am! I am looking for my daughter! Please help me!" He slammed his hand down on the counter in frus- tration. The lady on the other side of the counter put down her pen and picked up the picture. She stared at the picture for a few seconds. She had been at the desk the minute all hell broke loose, and she had been screamed at all morning. She understood the anxiety of being hurt and having to wait your turn, but this was a different anxiety for this man. He had completely lost his child.

The beast had claimed her, and she knew he was on the edge of a complete meltdown. She turned to one other person behind the counter and asked to please watch the desk for a minute. She walked around to where the couple was standing among the chaos. She still had the picture of Ariel in her hand when she reached them. "Sir, I…we will do everything we can to help you find your daughter. Let's go over here and you can tell me about how she became missing." She took them into the small chapel just off the main lobby waiting area and closed the door behind them. She noticed that the woman with this man seemed to be in a different world. "What's your name? And tell me about this little girl in the picture." He breathed a long sigh, finally someone was talking to him.

He still felt a barn-load of anxiety, but it seemed easier to handle with someone else's help. His wife sure wasn't helping at the moment. She was not mentally with them right now. "Her name is Ariel, she is our daughter. She is 5 years old. The tornado took her from my arms. Both of us were sucked out of our storm cellar and I simply didn't have the strength to hold on to her." He choked back the tears that he badly wanted to release but he decided it would be best for his wife if he maintained his composure. "I was tossed about 200 yards from our cellar. We looked all over the farm, but we couldn't find her. She is so tiny, so little, she doesn't weigh anything! I just should have been stronger is all. She would be with me now if I had hung on to her." He started to ramble a little and caught himself.

The admissions nurse sensed that he was about to lose it and put her hand on his shoulder. She believed strongly in the power of the human touch. She felt that it had its own healing power and she was giving her best shot at making this man and his wife feel better. She would worry about the wife in a moment but for now she needed to get more information from him. "Ariel is beautiful, and I am sure we are going to find her Mr.?" She drew the last part of that comment out in question form to keep the conversation going and not feel like an interrogation. "Patterson, I am Gerald Patterson, and this is my wife, Nancy." She rubbed his shoulder ever so slightly as sort of a way to congratulate him on calming down. "Mr. Patterson, we haven't had anyone that looks like your daughter come through here. We will certainly be on the lookout. Can you give me a number where I can reach you when we find her?" She was trying her best to help the young couple stay positive by saying "when" we find her instead of "if" we find her.

In her time in admissions she had seen parents lose all sense of reality and reason after they have lost a child. She knew that parents built their entire existence around their children and when that was taken away from them, they snapped. Empty nest was tolerable. At least the parents had time to prepare for the silence, but this was different. These were parents who lost their kids and may never see them again, much less touch them or hug them or cheer for them at a ballgame. This was a dangerous position. "Mr. Patterson, are you with me?" He seemed to have drifted off to the same place his wife was after he heard her tell them that they hadn't seen his little girl. "Mr. Patterson, I need you to stay with me, all right? The storm has passed, and we are still getting people in the ER. I am sure that we will find your daughter. Can you give me your number?" She was so focused on trying to keep them calm that she failed to remember that the attending physician, when the chaos broke out, had to divert some patients to the VA. It had totally slipped her mind.

Chapter 37

PAUL BLINKED HIS several times. The sunlight made it difficult for him to adjust but he managed to open his eyes, enough to see Jake kneeling over him. "Thought I had lost you, brother." Jake patted Paul on the chest when he said it. "I had to pound your cold heart into submission. You tried to check out on me. How do you feel, man?" Paul turned his head to the side to see Ariel lying next to him on the ground. It caused him a brief moment of panic which he didn't fully understand yet. He had only known this little girl for a few hours. He rolled over to reach her, but Jake stopped him. "Just hang on, man. She is breathing real slow. She has been asleep almost since the minute you took your tumble. Can you sit up?" The Boss moved his elbows up underneath himself so he could get enough leverage to begin the process of sitting up, but it was not easy. His chest still hurt.

He wasn't sure if it hurt because he thought he had had a heart attack or that maybe that big dumb cowboy Ranger had pounded on his chest. He managed to get himself into a sitting position, but Jake had to help him a little. "I remember seeing the bike and that was it, lights out, man." "Yeah, I think the shock of finding the bike may have been too much. I haven't had a chance to see how badly it's damaged. I kinda hate to look actually." Paul looked around to see if there was something he could grab to help him get up and found nothing. "Help me get to my feet, man. I can't just lay around enjoying the sun with a big dopey cowboy Ranger and a little girl. We need to see if the bike works." Jake helped him get to his feet. He was very wobbly and thought for second that he might just puke but he fought off the feeling. Jake bent down and picked Ariel up. Her head slumped over his shoulder. She was breathing very shallow. Jake felt helpless to help her. They took a few steps toward the motorcycle but before they could a good look at it... "It's not my bike. It's not Michele. It's is a nice bike, and someone is sure gonna miss it but it ain't mine, this one is a Panhead. See the rocker covers? Not a Knucklehead. Damn near the exact same paint job which I thought was original but obviously not now, that damn body shop screwed me over." Paul reached down to grab the handlebars to see if he could sit the bike up on its stand. Based on his present condition, that proved to be quite a challenge, but he managed to get it upright. It surprised him how little energy he had. Just yesterday he could have lifted the bike with one hand. Today was a much different story. The key was still in the ignition. "Do you mind trying the kick? I am not sure if I can make it happen right now." Jake started to throw his leg over the bike and try and kick it to life, but he realized that he had a little girl in his arms. "Can you hold her?" Paul reached out his arms and took a few steps closer to Jake, but he really wasn't sure if he even had the strength to hold this little girl. He decided he could do it and pulled Ariel close to him. She let out a small sigh when her head was on his shoulder again, almost as if she was happy to be back with him. It made him feel awkward, but he was happy for the thought. It was a good thought in a bad situation.

Jake got the bike balanced beneath him, turned the key, and gave it a kick. The bike came roaring to life like it was happy to be back in service. "This is one tough bike!" Jake was smiling ear- to-ear as he turned the throttle to test the RPM just a little. "Hop on the back, put her in between us. Can you hang on to me? Got the strength?" Paul shook his head in disgust at the thought of having to get on the back of a bike. As long as he was old enough to straddle an ass hammer he had never ridden on the back. It made him feel like a wuss to have to hold on to another dude and it made him feel like a bigger wuss to have to admit that he could and should. He was in no shape to muscle this Panhead out of this pasture and back on to a road. Paul took a deep breath and slung his leg over the back of the Panhead. He still had Ariel snugly against his chest. He tapped Jake on the shoulder. "Take it easy out of this pasture. I am not on as snug as I would like, and I don't want to lose my grip on her or you." Jake shook his head and gave the bike a little gas.

He knew which way he needed to go to meet up with the highway, but he wasn't sure how passable the pasture would be, so he went very slowly. He weaved his way through rocks and cactus, which seemed to be all the pasture was. He really didn't see anything that a cow could eat. The land seemed somewhat worthless to him. He was glad he lived in Dallas. He stopped the bike in order to check on his riders. "You all right?" Paul shook his head. "Yep, let's get this kid to a doctor. I can feel her heart beating against mine. Seems like it's about to pound out of her chest. Paul put his head down slightly to block the dust that was being kicked up and thought about that creature that told him there would be others. Collect what, he thought? What the hell does that mean? He never asked Jake if he saw it too.

Chapter 38

"SIR, HEAR IS THE SIDEARM for you. You will need to loop it through your belt." Mark's eyes got really big. "No thanks, Sergeant, I never carry a sidearm." Annemarie had positioned herself in one of the oversized chairs across from the two. "Lt., take the sidearm, that's an order." Mark reached out of more reflex than direction. She had a commanding way of getting people to do things. He was no exception. Once he had the weapon in his hand he had looked down at it and pulled it from the holster to at least see what he was dealing with. He didn't know much about guns, he never cared for them, but he knew the difference between a revolver and automatic.

This was obviously not a revolver. He realized even though he knew the difference, he did not know how to load, or unload this thing. Where was the safety? He had a million questions run through his mind. "Why do I need a gun?" Wally rolled his eyes, but Mark didn't catch him doing it, not that it mattered.

"I am not sure how many men we have detained, however, I know that one man who feels trapped and without options is a very dangerous formula. I also know that our extraction team is completely wiped." Mark shook his head.

The noise on the plane made it tough to catch all her words so he did the best lip-reading job he could do. "What does that mean...wiped?" Wally could tell that Mark was struggling to understand her over the noise, especially now since the landing gear was going down and the wind drag started adding to the already loud plane. "She means they don't exist, Lt. They are completely off the grid. Their fingerprints won't even come up at Langley. They could disappear, and nobody would know. They don't have social security numbers, they don't pay taxes, and when they die, they are buried in a non-descript Civil War grave where the record keeping of who was buried there was not good. It means if they wanted to cut your throat, my throat, and the General's, they could. They would disappear, and we would simply be listed as having been in a horrible plane crash of which there were no survivors and nothing recognizable of us left so mom, dad, brother, sister, and beloved Aunt Petunia can't have an open casket funeral for us. That's what it means."

Annemarie was bobbing her head up and down to show her compliance with Wally's assessment. "That's not possible! We can't have people who don't exist. That's the stuff movies are made from. That's simply not possible!" Mark was incredulous in his response. He was trying to process the information when he felt the wheels touch down. "Wally, make sure the weapon you just handed him is checked out and brief the Lt. on its action and safety features. Mar...uh, John, pay attention. Weapons haven't changed much since you were in ROTC, but they are a little easier to work with. It's important." She caught herself as she was about to call him Mark, but she caught herself and recovered quickly. "Lt., here is the safety, when you feel danger you can flick off from the holster, but I don't recommend that. You might shoot yourself in the leg. If you strike an artery, you'll have roughly three minutes to figure out a way to stop the bleeding or its hello Aunt Petunia. It's a slide action, here's how you jack around in the chamber. And here is how you eject and insert the clip. Easy as pie. Like the General said, no different than when you were in ROTC at Harvard."

Mark caught the sarcasm but didn't say anything. "Lt., we've dealt with this particular extraction team before. They aren't bad people but are excellent at what they do. But like any other human on the planet, power corrupts, and they know they are untouchable. It's a dangerous spot for anyone who has to deal with them. You stay close to me. The General can handle herself. Truth be known, I wouldn't fight her if I didn't have to. I might win just because I have more muscle mass, but she has more experience and she fights way dirty. I've seen it so I ain't worried about her." "Sergeant, people just can't be unaccountable. That's just not possible." Wally smiled a very sinister smile at him. "Don't be naïve, Sir. You really think a private wandering through a neighborhood in war-torn Iraq just happened to stumble on Saddam Hussein in a hole and WAHLAH!, we've captured one of the most brutal dictators in the world? You think that Gaddafi just got surprised and then overrun and a pole shoved up his ass for the entire world to see? He had more money than God, he could have flown out of that shithole at any time. Could have paid his pilot a million to keep it quiet and he'd be on Marlon Brando's tropical island with his pock-marked face and his pock-marked whores. People make those things happen long before they were deemed 'luck' or 'accidental'. The United States isn't the most powerful country on the planet by accident. Wise up, Sir." Mark looped the sidearm through his belt as earlier instructed.

His stomach felt very queasy. He now understood the mission a little better and the need for him to be in military clothes. His Brioni suits would probably not scare anyone. "What about Olivia – does she know?" Wally shook his head. "Negative, if she did, she'd never get on the plane. She is being given fatigues now with a minimal briefing from the co-pilot. She is to remain at the General's side at all times. Just so you know Lt., the code phrase is 'I always wanted to play a guitar'. If you hear that, get ready – the shit is about to hit the fan and you will need to become real proficient with that P320 you now have on your hip." The information coming at him was too much. He was having a very difficult time processing all of it. "What the hell is a P-3 whatever...?" Wally shook his head in amazement. "It's the gun you have, Sir. And by the way, never refer to it as a gun. It is your sidearm or your weapon, but it is not a gun." Mark was still processing the information. "What's the damn difference and who gives a shit?" Wally could tell he was upset. "Let's hope you won't have to figure that out, Sir, and the boys are in a good mood today." Wally unbuckled his seat harness and stood up. "Time to go, Sir."

Chapter 39

DR. HUNDLEE CLEARED THE TRIAGE area and was satisfied that they have survived the wave of patients created by the storm. She made her way up to trauma so she could help if needed. She knew from the way she had organized the triage area that trauma would be the most overloaded and overworked. The trauma ward was filled to capacity now. There were so many injured people from the tornado that they doubled-up in the rooms designed for one patient, and in some cases, put three in a room that was designed as a family suite. The space really wasn't the issue, the issue was electrical outlets. The rooms weren't designed to handle two and three heart monitors and IV drips, but with the help of maintenance and some handy use of electrical extension cords, they managed to handle it nicely. The maintenance team even taped down all the cords which seemed to be running everywhere so that they were not a trip hazard. She made a mental note to be sure and include the maintenance staff in any recognition ceremonies that were sure to come later. They certainly deserved it. They were working as hard as anyone in the hospital. She was quite proud of what this team of people was doing. She was amazed at how many patients they had packed into the trauma ward. She realized it should amaze her because she had seen way more logistical challenges overcome in Afghanistan. This was a piece of cake compared to that. Here, they just needed to work out the location of the internal injuries. That wasn't always easy, but it seemed a lot easier than trying to sew limbs back on when they were able or tracing the path of a bullet and repairing the damage as it ripped through the internal organs of a 19-year-old kid from Anywhere, USA.

Here there was a lack of blood, in Afghanistan there was blood everywhere. And, of course there, you didn't have children. She meticulously read the charts hanging outside of each door. She was impressed that even with the chaos of having so many patients arrive at once, the charts were very detailed, even the charts that were tacked to the doors outside the rooms that had three patients. The staff had not missed a beat. They were as proficient as any she had ever seen. What pulled on her biggest heart string was that some of the veterans who were being treated at the hospital began helping out as orderlies or maintenance, or anything that they could do to help the staff maintain control of the situation. She was always proud of being a veteran herself but watching some of these guys and ladies that were in the hospital throw themselves in despite some of their own pain really tugged at her heartstrings.

She saw one WWII vet sitting beside the bed of one of the patients that had a very swollen face, and he was simply holding his hand. He may not have been in great shape but the compassion he showed for a man he didn't know made her tear up. In her mind, society should see this. Society should see that kindness transcends generations. Maybe if people could really see what was going on in a time of crisis, we wouldn't have boys and girls go off to war and get blown apart in the name of religious hatred. The subject was far too deep and complicated for her to solve all by herself today. For now, she was needed as a doctor, not a philosopher.

She first checked the tall man who had no outward injuries but was in a coma. The CT came back and said that he had minor swelling around the brain. It could certainly be dangerous, but she had seen much worse. There was something else that was keeping this guy from waking up. All the medications seemed normal. The notes on the chart said he was found in his mangled truck. He had ID, but his name was not on the chart. The missing name was the first mistake she caught throughout this whole mess. Not bad, she thought. The chart did state that his relatives had been notified but none had arrived yet. She stood over him for a long time. He was a very big man, very broad frame. Her mother used to call frames like this "thick". His feet nearly dangled off the bed.

She gently tapped the backside of his hand with her pen to see if there was any reaction but got nothing. She exposed the bottom of his feet to see if she could provoke a tickle response but got nothing. She listened to his heart and found the beat to be normal. He was certainly an intriguing case but there would need to be more tests. She re-ordered a CT with contrast dye. Maybe they had missed something. She next moved to the man with the swollen face. The old veteran that she saw when she arrived was still there, holding this man's hand. "Hi, I am Doctor Hundlee, you aren't related to this patient, are you?" The veteran tried to get up and greet her, but he was really struggling to get to his feet. "Oh, don't get up, please. You are doing more good holding his hand than you would be shaking mine." The old veteran had a hat on that said WWII Navy Veteran at the top, and at the bottom, beneath what looked to be a boat, read in bright yellow stitch-ing: USS Batfish. "No, ma'am, I am not related, but when they finished popping him with those electrodes, it looked to me like he was in a world of trouble. I didn't want him to go off and meet his Maker alone. I guess I just felt bad for him. I wouldn't want to be alone if it were my last hours." She felt the tears begin to well up in her eyes but fought them back so she could maintain a professional demeanor. "I couldn't agree more. You are very kind for staying with him. I am sure he appreciates it and I know I do." The veteran settled back into his chair but never let go of his hand. "He seems to be a little better. For just a spilt second there I swore he tightened his grip on my hand. Real quick like. I can't be sure though. I am pretty old, and I don't trust my own reflexes anymore."

She smiled at him. She wanted so badly to give him a hug and maybe she would after she was done. This man deserved a medal for his compassion. She looked down at him as she was reaching for her stethoscope.

Getting a read on his pupils would be tough as he had been intubated to keep his throat from swelling shut. Surgical incisions had been made just under his right cheekbone and just above his left ear to help ease the tension on his skin. The X- rays showed that he had two fractured orbital sockets, a broken jaw, and a skull fracture. It appeared to her that he had slammed head-first through a car windshield or something. He would probably not remember any of what has happened to him today. When he woke up, and she was very confident that he would wake up eventually, he would never know that he was resuscitated twice. Along with the head injuries, it was discovered that he had a collapsed lung, actually it was more of a punctured lung. The impact had broken nearly all his ribs which caused one to break off and puncture a hole in his left lung. The stress on his body and brain caused his heart to go into cardiac arrest. He was lucky to be alive.

The paramedics had done a great job of keeping him alive during transit because the chart showed he went into cardiac arrest in transit. The trauma surgeon that worked on him in the trauma ER not only brought him back to life, but also made the incisions on his face and head in locations that he would eventually watch disappear with time. Had he not made the cuts on his face to ease the tension on his skin, his skin may have literally burst open, which would leave scars that never went away. She went through the same procedures as she had done with the tall patient, she tried to provoke a response through slight stimulation, but got none. She knew she might have to wait until this guy's swelling went down before she could see any rapid eye movement.

She thought he was lucky to be in a coma, he would be in a great deal of pain if he were not. She felt bad for him. When he woke up he would not want to see his face. He looked to be in good shape and at this point she couldn't tell if he was a good-looking guy or not, but he had some very nice and colorful artwork on his arms all the way down to his wrists. She believed they called them "sleeves". She wasn't a tattoo expert for certain, but she could tell this stuff was high quality, very defined and very colorful. That kind of work must have cost him a pretty penny. That angel on his arm was amazing all by itself. She looked at his chart and the notes at the bottom read: John Doe, No ID Available.

She moved from room to room. She checked charts then checked pupils, heartbeat, breathing, medication and a whole list of other little checks that she had mastered from her days in the military and here at the VA. She shook some hands and visited with some families that had already arrived. She was amazed at the spirit of people. Everyone that she met wanted to help and couldn't be nicer if they tried. She was about to make the L when she ran into the head trauma surgeon that had been on this floor when all hell broke loose. He was the man in her eyes. He had done some amazing stuff in the last few hours. She had no idea how many lives he had saved by his quick thinking and calm reactions. "Dr. Washburn, nice work up here." As she said it, he stuck out his hand to shake hers, but she gave him a hug instead. She believed strongly in the power of the human touch and this man had just saved the lives of several people and he needed to know she admired and appreciated him. He certainly didn't shy away from the embrace as the two stood locked together for a few minutes. She swears to this day, she actually felt the stress lift from his shoulders and vanish into thin air. He was clearly on edge and she had just delivered what the doctor needed, not ordered. "Thank you, Dr. Hundlee, I was just doing my job." She laughed as they broke the hug. She still had her hand on his shoulder though. There was that touch thing. "Just doing your job, my ass. From what I can see and have been told, you were Clark Kent unmasked up here. There is an orderly downstairs that swears you stepped into a phone booth somewhere up here." He laughed and blushed a little when she said it. Dr. Washburn was certainly not in the profession for the attention.

He was as quiet, steady, and methodical as you could ever ask anyone to be. He was a little awkward with his bedside manner but that was because he tended to focus so much on the problem and listening to what the patient said that he failed to engage them in any small talk. She thought he kind of reminded her of one of those Ghostbusters on TV. The guy version, not the girl version, she couldn't remember exactly which one. "That must have been the orderly that was in the room when the little girl and the guy crashed in the same room at the same time. It was a bit hectic, but the nurses actually did a phenomenal job of keeping that little girl alive. Is that orderly ok? He seemed a bit freaked out by all of it. You know, for a second when I got into the room, I swear he was about to give that guy CPR. I am not sure it would have helped him, but I was impressed that he was in a room full of medical professionals and was willing to jump in and try. We should make sure he gets his proper recognition." She laughed when he described the scene in detail. "Hey, I was about to go check on the only two women on this floor, the little girl that we hit with adrenalin and a woman that has some burns on the left side of her body. She is perplexing. Actually, they both are. They are stable, but both are still reluctant to wake up. Would you mind joining me?" Michelle nodded her head, smiled, and said, "After you, Doctor".

Chapter 40

SHE SAT THERE IN THE CHAPEL with her husband and the admissions lady. She heard everything that was being said but had no desire to add to the conversation. She couldn't get the image out of her head. She replayed it over and over until she was sick of seeing it. Every time she replayed it she saw herself grabbing them both and pulling them back into the shelter. The questions came by the thousands. She couldn't stop them, and she couldn't slow them down. Worse was that she couldn't answer any of them. Why was she not taken? Why did the storm not touch their house? Did the storm target that little storm cellar door specifically? Why did her husband come back and not Ariel? Why did he not hang on to her? Why? Why? Why?

She just wanted the questions that continued to stab her brain like so many daggers to stop but they wouldn't. She was afraid if she spoke she would say something she regretted. She had lost her little baby girl. The hospital didn't know where she was. She was so little and so helpless! Why did he let her go? Why did she marry him against her father's wishes? She tried with all her might to fight that last one off, but it continued to wedge itself in between every other question that had just beaten her head like a blacksmith pounding away his hot iron. God, please help me. I can't get through this anymore. I want it to end. She heard the admissions nurse tell her husband that they didn't have anyone that fit Ariel's description.

Why was he so weak? Why couldn't the storm have just let them go? Why didn't it get the neighbor's farm? They weren't good people; they deserved to be punished but not her. Why did God make storms anyway? Who the hell needed them? What good did they do? Rain would have been just fine but why does God make it so violent? Was there really a God? If there really were a true and just God, he wouldn't be so cruel as to take a little girl and toss her into the belly of this beast! She could hear her father now, I told you not to marry him. I told you he was not a worthy husband. I told you he was weak. You see! He couldn't even protect his own daughter.

Please, God, make the questions stop! I love him. He did his best. Please don't do this to me. "Honey, honey, do you have your cell phone?" He didn't have one. He never needed one. He was a farmer and was in the field all day. If anyone needed him, they knew where to find him. He had bought one for his wife though because her father chewed his ass out one day for not giving his little girl a way to call for him for emergencies. He took the ass chewing because he loved his wife more than life itself. He always took the abuse her father dished out. It was his way of sacrificing for her and keeping the peace. He knew that any open riff between him and her father would upset his wife and he just wasn't willing to put her through that misery. Luckily, he didn't have to see her father very often but when he did, he hated it. "Honey, I need your cell phone, do you have it?" Nancy sort of snapped out of her fog for a second, at least long enough to place her hand in her purse that was sitting beside her and fumbled around for the phone. Gerald took the phone and handed it to the admissions nurse. "Mr. Patterson, I just need a number, not the phone." He smiled at her. "I don't know the number. I thought maybe you could call your cell phone and it would tell you what number it is." She smiled and opened the phone. Luckily it wasn't a smartphone. It was a flip phone with no code to open it. She dialed her own cell phone number and waited for it to reach her voicemail so she would know for sure that call went through.

When she heard her own voice, she closed the phone shut and handed it back to him. "Ok, that should do it. I have your number now and I will be sure and call you the minute I find your daughter." "You're not going to find her. She has been taken away from us and we are not going to ever see her again." Nancy was still in her trance when she said it. It sent chills up the nurse's spine. Gerald lowered his head and started to cry. "Mrs. Patterson, you can't think that way. It's still early, we will find your daughter. Please pull yourself together." She shifted her focus to Mrs. Patterson completely. She put her hand in the middle of her back and softly rubbed it. She made a sort of circular motion with the gentle rubbing. "Honey, I am going to find you a doctor, ok? Just sit right here and wait and I will be right back." She was really worried that this woman had already snapped. Mr. Patterson was trying to hold it together and was doing quite well, she thought, until Mrs. Patterson said that. "Mr. Patterson, stay here with your wife. We are going to find some help for both of you. Stay with me, ok?" He never looked up at her, he just continued to sob. She patted Mr. Patterson on the shoulder and walked out of the room. She needed to find a doctor really fast for these folks. She would call the county sheriff's office too. Maybe they had some more information.

It still didn't occur to her that the VA had patients too. Gerald wiped the tears from his eyes with his sleeve. He looked at Nancy. She was so distant. She was so far away. He knew he had lost her just as sure as he had lost their baby. He stood up from the chapel bench they were sitting on and kissed her on the forehead. He felt the back of his pants to see if it was still there. No point in saying much now. "I love you, Nancy". He turned and walked out of the chapel. It was time to pay what he owed. It was time to atone for his mistake and he knew it.

Chapter 41

IT WAS PITCH BLACK WHEN the four of them stepped off the plane. One of the pilots came back to the cargo area before the plane even came to a stop and was briefing them on a bunch of stuff, but Mark paid them no attention. He was still pissed at hearing they were in a dangerous spot; he had been given a damn gun to carry around like some sort of Wild West moron. He could even hear the spurs jingling as he walked. Good Lord what had he gotten himself into? This was stupid. He was not a soldier and should not be carrying a gun. He corrected his inner thoughts and said "weapon" instead of "gun". He didn't want GI Joe Wally or whatever the hell his name was to get pissed and decide to put a bullet into his head. The thoughts were swirling. He glanced at Olivia through what little light the plane door gave off and noticed her eyes were puffy. She had obviously been crying after her little briefing. Mark wondered if they had told her that she could disappear too. They stood there on the tarmac with one of the pilots as he continued to brief Wally and Annemarie.

Mark wasn't sure how many pilots it took to fly this plane. He had not met anyone on the crew but assumed the crew knew what was going on. They had to have had some serious security clearance already in order to fly onto this airstrip, and they had to be damn good pilots because as far as Mark could tell, there were no runway lights. Maybe this was just a test. His best friend and the President of the United States wanted to see how loyal he was.

Olivia walked up to Mark and gave him a hug. He was a bit unnerved by it because it wasn't solicited. She was certainly a pretty woman and he didn't mind the attention, but she was too young. "I felt badly like I needed to be touched. I needed to feel human. Don't worry, I mean nothing by it, you just seemed like the least threatening person of my current choices." Mark released her embrace. "I will take that as a compliment" he said. "Are you ok?" She smiled at him; he was struck by how perfect her teeth were and that she could easily do a toothpaste commercial. "No, I am not. I am not supposed to be here. I am supposed to be back in Atlanta with my boyfriend. I am supposed to be snuggled up to him right now. He doesn't even know where I am. They wouldn't give me a chance to let anyone know where I was going or what I was doing. All they said was 'we will take care of it'. They even took my phone from me. When I protested, they threw my contract at me. I didn't understand what my contract had to do withanything, but they told me I had signed a contract that permitted them to close all communications in case of an emergency. I read that part too, but I thought that meant that I would have to keep my mouth shut if something went wrong inside the building. I could do that, you know. I could keep my mouth shut. I wouldn't say a word but hate worrying right now in the middle of all this that other people are now worried about me! They don't even know where I am!" Her voice continued to rise as she became more nervous and agitated.

Mark stepped forward and grabbed her again. He pulled her close to him and hugged her as tight as he dared. She started sobbing as she buried her head in his chest. "Honey, you have to get it together. You are here for a reason. If you lose it, we all lose it." He tried to find the right words to calm her down but hell, he was just as scared. "You don't understand. If you get one whiff of that virus they have inside that building, you will be dead in less than 24 hours. More than likely you will be dead in 10 minutes, but certain people can incubate the virus for 23

hours before they feel anything and in the 24th hour, you are dead." Mark remembered her quick briefing on the plane to Annemarie. He had read the report on the strain. In that report they had nicknamed the virus Dracula because of the way it drained the blood. It gave Mark the creeps just reading about it in the report. "We are going to be just fine. You need to dry up and buck up." That was his dad coming out of him.

His dad was full of those catchy sayings from his days in the oil field. "You have to promise me that if you see my eyes turn deep purple, you'll put a bullet in my head. That is the beginning of the end and it is more pain than anyone could imagine. And I don't want to die in this ridiculous uniform. I look like shit." Annemarie walked up after her and Wally had a private conversation. "What's going on here?" Mark shook his head as if to proclaim that nothing was going on.

He actually felt like he had just been caught cheating on his one true love, even though she had no idea he was in love with her. At least that's what he thought. "Nothing, ma'am, we are just both gathering our nerves a little." Olivia pulled away and wiped her eyes with the cuff of her fatigues. Mark had not even noticed until she said it that she was in fatigues just like everyone else now. He did notice that she did not have a gun. Perhaps she made Wally too nervous to give her one. Maybe she refused to call it a "weapon" and he gave up. "Ok, through that hangar is a set of double doors. You have to code- in with your badge and we can only enter one at a time. Your badge works, it's been tested long before I gave it to you, yours too, Olivia. After you are scanned through the double doors, you will go through a series of manned checkpoints. At the first checkpoint the MP will ask for your ID from DOD. You both have one in your breast pocket. He will then do a retinal scan. Once he has a retinal scan and a left middle fingerprint, he will load you into the system and you won't need your ID anymore. You can put it away." Mark and Olivia both were trying pay attention, but it seemed like all they needed to do was get through the first double doors like they were water draining out of a bath tub. There was only one place you could go. "And after that?" Mark was quick to ask the question. He knew Olivia would be thinking the same thing. Wally walked up at that moment. "After that, Olivia will remain at the General's right flank and you will remain on my left flank. Don't wander off and don't interject unless the General prompts you." Wally seemed very relaxed as if he was happy to be in the middle of a dangerous situation. "I wish I could play the guitar." Olivia had obviously been briefed as Mark had. She still had a little humor left in her and it made Mark smile. Wally actually smiled too. "I am glad you paid attention, Ms. Millben, let's hope you never have to learn unless you really want to." Annemarie looked at Olivia as if she was looking for something. "Olivia, did you forget something?" Olivia's eyes got big and she said, "Oh, shit. I will be right back." She darted back up the cargo ramp. She returned a few minutes later with a case that looked like an oversized brief case. Annemarie seemed to read Mark's mind. "It's a 181 containment case and suit. She will be the only one allowed to handle the vials that we have recovered." Once they were satisfied that they had all the equipment they needed, they each made their way inside the hangar and through the double doors. It was everything and more of what Mark expected. Taxpayer dollars at their finest. This place was amazing.

Chapter 42

DR. WASHBURN WALKED INTO THE ROOM where the two women were. Saying the little girl was a woman was just easier in a conversational way. He turned to make sure that Dr. Hundlee was still trailing along; she was a few paces behind as she stopped to grab the charts. Dr. Hundlee was struck by the toughness of both girls. Both had basically expired and fought their way back to life. The defibrillator and the adrenalin may have helped them, but they were alive because their bodies chose to fight. The woman had been burned by electricity. She must have touched a live wire or something because she was burned on her hand and the electricity had chosen to exit out her elbow, but while it was searching for the path of least resistance, it blew her pinky off. Her hair was badly singed and, in some cases, it had fallen out in clumps. The pain must have been excruciating if she felt it. The shock was severe enough to cause her heart to stop.

The nurse in the room when they walked in smiled at both of them. "She woke up for just a few seconds. She tried to open her eyes and I think she actually tried to speak but didn't realize she was intubated. We made a note on the chart of the time and duration it happened, Dr. Washburn." He had already taken his penlight out and was examining her pupils. Once again, his focus on the patient left the nurse feeling unheard or ignored. Dr. Hundlee recognized her body language and acknowledged her professionalism and diligence to make up for Dr. Washburn's inattentive behavior. "Thank you, I see that notated here in the chart. That was just an hour ago." Dr. Washburn was now listening to her heart and timing her pulse. "Her pupils are normal, she is responding to light stimulation. Her lungs are normal. I think we can remove the tube." Michelle continued to read. The chart said when the paramedics arrived she was not breathing. Michelle thought she must have been very lucky to be alive. She flipped the pages of the chart and was satisfied she had all the information she needed about this patient.

She set the chart down on the counter and shifted her attention to the little girl's chart. She too had stopped breathing. A motorist out along FM 2176 surveying the damage of the tornado found her where it intersects with Loop 335. Luckily for her the motorist was an LPN at Northwest and knew how to administer CPR on a child. She had some swelling just above her left temple. She made it to the hospital only to crash again. This time Dr. Washburn used adrenalin to get it restarted. It was a bold move to use on a child this small. He calculated the odds of survival with the needle or the paddles, and he chose the needle. It turned out for now to be the exact right move. "We still don't have any ID on the little girl." The nurse spoke up again. "Based on her condition, and the fact that no one has been here looking for her, I fear her parents might be dead." Michelle took that in for a minute. "I doubt anyone would be looking at the VA for a little girl. Have we informed the sheriff's department and the media that we have a little girl at the VA?" The nurse turned flush at the suggestion. She knew it was simple common sense yet somehow, she had not thought that angle through. "My goodness, Doctor, I feel so stupid for not thinking to do that hours ago." Michelle smiled and started to say something but was interrupted by Dr. Washburn. "You shouldn't feel stupid. You were focused on doing your job. There is a PR/ Media staff here at the hospital that should have already handled that for us. You have done a wonderful job handling the pressure of all of this." Michelle continued to smile. Perhaps Dr. Washburn has a better bedside manner than she had given him credit for.

The nurse gushed at the compliment and left the room. She was already on her way to the offices where the HR, PR, and Media groups resided. She was about to light a fire under them. Once the nurse had left the room, Michelle dropped all the formalities of office protocol. "They seem stable, Scott. Why do I sense some concern? Your body language is sending signals that you aren't comfortable with their current conditions." Dr. Washburn loved it when she dropped the formalities. In fact, he loved it when everyone dropped the formalities, and he understood the need for a clear hierarchy, but not in all situations. Even though he had paid his dues through medical schools and internships at both Johns Hopkins and UCLA, he had done the stint where he didn't sleep for 36 hours and then was only able to catch a nap in a vacant room. Through all that, he hated the doctors who felt like they had to be addressed as DOCTOR. So what if someone wanted to call him Scott? Hell, that was his name and as far as he knew, it was the only thing that had ever been given to him his whole life and he was proud of it. He knew what they said about him, that he was a little cold and aloof, but that couldn't be further from the truth. He loved people, but he loved being a doctor even more. He loved solving problems and fixing things. Sometimes, simple conversations got in the way of his work and he was criticized for it. His wife loved him, his kids loved him, and he didn't really care much what people said. In the end, he knew what he stood for and he was a very good doctor. "I don't think that I am as concerned now as I was a few hours ago. I am concerned about these two and the guys across the hall. You know, the big one and the one with the swollen head seem to be different than all the rest. Those four have crashed multiple times. Each time they crash and are brought back, their vitals improve dramatically. Not just a little but dramatically. In fact, their vitals are actually better than some of the others that are on this floor that are up walking around and talking to people. I am not concerned, I am simply perplexed. It is like they don't want to come back. Craziest thing I've ever seen, Michelle." Michelle hadn't thought anything like that. She thought that he was concerned that they were not out of the woods, not that they didn't want to come out of the woods. "I see, hadn't thought of it that way. What would you like to do?" He intertwined his fingers together and tapped his thumbs together. He tended to do that when he was stumped or nervous. He certainly wasn't nervous in this case, but he was sure stumped. "I would like to have someone with them all the time. The monitors are great, but I want someone to monitor eyelids and body movement if there is any. You know, just sit and pay attention, make notes and let me know what they see. They may not see a damn thing and it will be boring as hell for now. That's about all I can think of. Any thoughts? What am I missing?" Michelle was a damn good doctor in her own right, but she knew he was better. She thought she didn't have anything of substance to add. "I can arrange that for sure. I am with you; their charts show marked improvement after each cardiac arrest. I just can't wrap my head around why they continue the myocardial reactions they are having when all indicators say they should be getting better. There is no real reason, especially the little one. Her heart is strong as a grizzly bear." They were about to leave the room when they heard her soft faint voice. "I'm so thirsty."

<h1 style="text-align:center">Chapter 43</h1>

"TEN HUT" IS WHAT IT SOUNDED LIKE but even Mark knew it was the military's aggressive way to say "attention". Wally made her presence known as they entered the room as was customary when traveling with an Officer. There were at least twenty men in uniform, black uniforms, in the first room. "Wally! I see you are still carrying the General's luggage. You will make a great bellhop when you are finished being a toy soldier." Wally continued walking towards the voice until he was standing in front of the colonel. He yanked a crisp salute to the colonel. Although he would love it in this case, he would never break military protocol. He was a soldier in all weathers, good and bad. "At ease, Wally." The colonel said and returned a salute that was not nearly as sharp as Wally's. Wally relaxed. "Colonel Dickhead, it is always a pleasure to see you. It reminds me of how fucked up the military can be when it wants to. You're Uncle Sam's version of Affirmative Action. You help Uncle Sam meet his quota of retards with a bird on their collar." One of the colonel's loyal recruits took offense to Sergeant Wallace's blatant disrespect for the colonel and started to take an aggressive step towards Wally. "Son, unless you want your beloved colonel's bird pinned to your forehead, I'd stand down." The colonel seemed to enjoy the banter but decided he'd take it up a notch. "Sergeant Major, I'd like to see you try to remove my birds." He took a step closer to Wally. Mark was in the back of the room watching this. He figured they would never get to transport the virus back to Atlanta because they were all about to die. "Colonel, as an enlisted man, it would mean a stretch at Leavenworth should I remove your insignia however, I intend to ram you completely up the ass of the eager corporal here until your pin gently reaches his forehead."

Annemarie heard the last part and knew she had brought the right man along. "That's enough, gentlemen. Your brains are needed here, not your testosterone. We have a situation that could wipe out all of Texas with one turn of the screw and you guys want to measure dicks? Give me a fuckin' break! Where are the subjects you collected and where is the vial, Colonel?" She wasn't screwing around when she said it.

Mark was fascinated with the way the whole room reacted. It was almost as if she had neutered every man in the room. The egos deflated and so did the aggression, at least temporarily. "Inside here we dispense with protocol. Now move, gentlemen! Where is my damn bug?" The colonel's men all scrambled which was a sign that she had just taken control of his team without even brandishing a weapon, badge, or aggression. Yes, Mark was in love. He wanted this woman. She was a bad ass. She was his bad ass as far as he was concerned.

They all made their way through another set of double doors. Not counting the retinal scan station, Mark guessed this was their 5th door to go through. When they walked through the last set of doors, it opened up into a mix between a lab and barracks area. Each of the detainees had been laid out in their bunks. All were on their backs, handcuffed to the bed, and had a continuous fluid drip in each of them so they would stay hydrated during their prolonged hibernation. All the drips were auto-fed so there was only a need to insert the needle. After that, the lab director could control any station with any drug he chose. "General, welcome to our control room. I am sure you want to know where the vial is being kept. It has been safely stored and we are currently in no danger. None of the subjects have shown any signs of incubation, contamination, or eruption. Would you like me to wake them up? Each is being administered small doses of Propofol. If I slowly reduce the amount they will wake up rather quickly." He smiled as he said it. Mark thought the guy was a bit too smarmy for his taste. "Not necessary. I want to speak to a Jack Ingle. Which one is he?" The smarmy guy fiddled with the chart. "He is the one at the far end. I am reducing his Propofol and switching to a modest dose of Sodium Thiopental." He kind of wrung his hands when he said it. His motions and demeanor made Mark think about that mad scientist that he has seen in old movies that screams "it's alive". What a dork, he thought. Annemarie had the same thought that Mark had, what the hell was that, Sodium Thiopental? Olivia must have read Mark's mind; she whispered in his ear, "Truth Serum". Mark felt like he needed to write this down as if he was in Chemistry 101. She continued, "It doesn't always work. In fact, I would never trust it." Mark continued to shake his head like he understood completely. In reality, he saw it work on TV, why the hell wouldn't it work now?

Annemarie walked towards where a peacefully resting Jack Ingle was laying, totally unaware of his surroundings. His eyes flickered as if they were following the end of an old movie reel. Once they stopped flickering, he had this very nasty stare. Mark could see it from across the room when he lifted his head, tried to sit up, and realized he was locked down with some cuffs and leather straps. When he spoke, he was groggy sounding, but it became clearer and stronger with every curse word. "Someone better let me the fuck out of this monkey fucking trap now!" Annemarie sat on the bed beside him. Mark was not concerned about the man in the bunk; he kept his eye on the crazy colonel. The colonel seemed to stay directly behind Annemarie. Mark felt like he was hovering and maybe even plotting. What was always reassuring to Mark was that Sergeant Brian Wallace was always very close by and it also seemed that Sergeant Brian Wallace was prepared for everything. "Mr. Ingle, I have some questions for you." Apparently, he wasn't in the mood for questions. "Fuck you, bitch. I don't give a shit what you want. Get me out of this fuckin' psycho trap or I will kill your butch ass." Annemarie remained calm and showed little reaction to his vulgarity. It didn't faze her at all. "Mr. Ingle, it has always been my impression that you biker types were anti- social, long on nerve, but woefully short on brains. You have adequately confirmed my suspicions." Mark couldn't help but chuckle. He wasn't the only one in the room who found her retort effective and humorous. "What the fuck are you talking about, bitch?"

Annemarie placed her hand on his chest as if she was his mother saying goodnight to him. "Well, you see, you have this needle in your arm, it is an auto-feed. It works on voice command. It is truly amazing technology. All I have to say is something like, oh hell, what's the name of that shit they use...?" She turned to the mad scientist. "Commander, what is it I am thinking of?" The mad scientist smiled his creepy smile. "Well it could be Sodium Thiopental, but I just weaned him off of that, it causes a nice deep sleep. Oh, I know! You're thinking of the cocktail of Pentobarbital, which induces unconsciousness; followed by Pavulon which causes muscle paralysis and respiratory failure, and lastly my personal favorite, which is Potassium Chloride, which then stops the old ticker. It's not really necessary though. That respiratory failure will kill you but it's kind of painful." Annemarie looked at Mr. Ingle with the most serious look Mark had ever seen. "In other words, all I have to do is say 'put this moron to sleep' and that's it. End of story, no more motorcycles, no more patches, no more women, and no more love. You see, you are tied up, got nowhere to go, you don't know where you are, and no one knows you are here. You will be our version of Jimmy Hoffa. Throw another temper tantrum and I will give the order. Now I know that you think I'm just a dumb bitch, but at the moment, this dumb bitch holds your balls and your life in my hands." For effect, she cupped his crotch and squeezed just a little.

It must have been enough to get his attention because he became a totally different person. "General, if you were in my position, you'd do the same thing." Annemarie took her hand off his nads and patted him on the chest again. "Good point, you know your insignia?" He seemed to relax. He laid his head back on the pillow. "I was a Marine, ma'am. 67 and 68, MEF and hated every second of it." Annemarie turned to the colonel. "Untie this Marine, Colonel. I would like to talk to him without the restraints." "General, I don't recommend that." "That's an order, Colonel." She turned to look at the mad scientist. "Come take this needle out of his arm." She looked around the room as if she was looking for something then she made eye contact with Mark. "Lt. Holmes, come over here. Olivia, you too." Annemarie turned her attention back to the now untied Jack Ingle. He was still laying on the bed though.

He appeared to still be a little woozy. "What was your rank, Mr. Ingle?" He tried to sit up and she helped pull him forward so that he could. "Lance Corporal, ma'am." She smiled at that response. Mark saw her go from cut throat smart-ass to the most compassionate woman he'd ever seen. It was amazing to watch. "Well Lance Corporal Ingle, I am General Annemarie Dobson. I have some questions about your cargo today."

Chapter 44

JAKE KEPT THE BIKE under control. He was surprised at how well a street bike was handling this pasture. Every now and then he would hit a fresh cow turd and the bike would slide a bit, but he had learned what to watch out for. He wanted to hurry but he knew that Paul was in a very perilous way. His breathing was bad. He could feel Ariel against his back, wedged between himself and Paul, and she didn't seem to be in much better shape. He hadn't told either of them but seeing that creepy thing next to Paul when Paul went down with his heart attack or whatever it was caused him his own issues. He got very dizzy and had a hard time getting to Paul while carrying the little girl. He had this constant ringing in his ears that he couldn't shake loose. He remembered his granddad had hearing aids and when the little batteries would die they would let off this high pitch squeal and everyone in the room could hear it except his granddad. Someone always had to yell at him to go change his batteries.

It made him happy to reflect on his granddad. His granddad was a revered man in his day. He was a Texas Ranger too. In fact, the reason Jake went into law enforcement was his granddad. He remembered getting all dressed up when his granddad was inducted into the Texas Ranger Hall of Fame. It was a big deal to him then and it was an even bigger deal to him now. He was proud of his family name in Texas law enforcement. He was always a very methodical and consistent Ranger. He never missed a detail and was never afraid to get his hands dirty in the process. He could mix it up with any-one, it didn't matter what his size was, and he was fearless. It also didn't hurt that his granddad stood 6 feet 6 inches tall and was as wide as the doorframe. Jake had almost the same frame except Jake was 6 feet 4 inches.

His granddad received a lot of recognition for his work at keeping the peace and keeping people from getting killed during the Lonestar Steel Strike in 1968. The strike lasted nearly nine months and tensions were very high. He tried to channel his memories of his granddad through himself to help get these people out of this stupid cow pasture that he really had no idea how he got into, but more importantly, get them and himself away from those creepy things that show up and talk about collecting. That stuff scared the shit out of him. He thought if he headed straight East, he would run into I-25 at some point, or at least find some paved road so they could travel considerably faster than they were. No matter how slowly they were going, it was still progress. To Jake, they had been spinning their wheels for a long time.

That was another thing that struck him as he felt the small breeze in his face; he had no concept of time. It seemed as though the sun had not moved in the sky at all, but surely, they had been out here in the middle of the deserted Panhandle for at least six hours. So much had happened, yet the sun had not moved. He tried to push that thought out of his head because it just made him uneasy. That was another thing. He had a watch on when he left for the day and now it was gone. Maybe when the truck spun out of control he lost it and didn't know it. Neither he nor Paul had a cell phone. Paul said his phone was in his saddlebags. And Ariel was just a little girl, lost and scared, and had latched on to Paul and wasn't going to let go. His mind was in hyper drive.

He could still feel Ariel breathing against his back, which was a good sign. He was worried about her. She was so tiny. He finally ran into what he figured he would eventually run into, a barbed wire fence. He slowed the bike down to a stop. That wasn't very hard, they were barely moving. The terrain had become less cow shit and more rocks. He hit the kill switch and kicked the stand in place. He could feel Paul's head leaning against his back. "Are we there?" Jake had to chuckle at that one. "I wish. We are at a barbed wire fence. We need something to cut it with or something to knock it over. I feel like we are so close to the loop. We just need to get past this fence. You're gonna have to lean back a little so I can get up. You all right, man?"

Paul had been battling to stay upright on the entire ride. If Ariel hadn't somehow become his responsibility, he felt like he would have just fallen off and been done with it. His chest hurt so badly. He was weak and was having trouble breathing. He had never felt this bad in his entire life. He forced his head off Jake's back, which felt like he was lifting a boulder with no hands. He held tight to Ariel. His bond had become way more than he ever expected. He felt like he had known her for all her short little life. This was all new territory for him. He certainly was capable of love. He loved Renee more than life itself. He badly needed to get back to her and tell her that. He was lousy at telling her he loved her. He knew she knew it and he tried to show her as much as he knew how but just saying it was very hard for him. Somehow in one day, he had fallen in love with a little girl who up until now talked all the time.

That was bothering him too; he had no idea what time it was. He didn't have his phone and never wore a watch, so he had no idea what time it was. It seemed as though the sun had not moved in the sky. He felt like they had been stuck out here in the middle of nowhere forever but there was still plenty of sun in the sky. He just wanted to get back to Renee and get this little girl back to her parents. He wondered if his guys were ok.

Were they scattered all over the Panhandle too? That tornado had picked him up, so it surely had picked up a few others. He hoped they were ok.

He hoped that Jack had the sense to keep moving. That cargo had to be in California soon and it was a huge payday. This shipment was going to set him and Renee up for the rest of their lives. He knew Renee had all that money and didn't need any money from him, but at least this way, he could bring something more to the table than the nickels and dimes he had been. He knew the cargo wasn't a drug as usual. He wasn't clear on what it was, even though he had tried to extract that information from the buyers, he got nowhere with it and didn't want to press the subject too much. After all, they were paying his team almost 4 million dollars for the transportation. It was the biggest score they had ever had. The club would get 2 million and he would get almost 2 million alone. That was the arrangement since he had set it all up. This was a deal he had worked on for almost a year and frankly, he was happy that it was almost over.

Now things had changed. His bike was gone and that is where half of the stuff was. He and Jack decided to split the cargo in half so that if something happened to either one of them, at least they would get half a payday. He had no idea who the real buyer was because they had only talked on the phone. He knew they were Indian. Not the Native American kind but the kind that were actually from India. He wasn't sure if India was the right country, but he knew they were from that area and they weren't very pleasant people to deal with. They always seemed angry but nevertheless, they paid very well. He was sure they were a legitimate contract because they had already up-fronted them 900K in good faith money.

Paul was surprised at the size of the payday. His crew had been drug runners as long as he could remember and had never been paid like this and had never received upfront money of almost a million dollars. They didn't deal directly with the customer on the street, which he liked very much. He likened his team to a freight company like JB Hunt, except JB Hunt drivers didn't go to prison when they were pulled over. This was going to be his last haul. He had seen enough violence. Hell, he had participated in enough violence to last him a lifetime. He had already discussed it with the Board and he was stepping down as President when they returned. This payday would take care of him and Renee for a very long time. They could start a family, which he wanted very badly now that he had felt what it was like to have a young life completely dependent upon him. It was scary to think that if he wanted to, he could leave her with the cops when he got to where he was going. They would probably stick her in one of those children's homes where they were just a number. In no way was he going to let that happen. If he didn't find her parents, she was going to stay with him and Renee. Renee would make an excellent mom and he was way ready to find out. Jesus, he felt bad, but he was battling through it. He had to. He had too much left to do.

Chapter 45

GERALD MADE HIS WAY out of the chapel. He glanced at the statue of the Virgin Mary that seemed to be staring directly at him. He stood still for a second and gave her a serious look back. He thought about all that he had been through in the last 24 hours. Life was full of twists, turns, and ups and downs. Today was all twists and all downs. The downs were as bad as he imagined anyone had ever gone through. Maybe it was selfish on his part and he should be tougher, but this was unbearable. He felt the weight of the entire world on his shoulders and didn't have the strength to carry it around. He blew a kiss to her as she stared so strongly and lovingly back at him. He mouthed the words I'm sorry to her and exited the chapel.

The lobby wasn't as chaotic as it had been when they arrived. He saw that there was a new admissions dude at the window. Since there was currently no one at the window, he decided it was worth a shot to ask again. "Hey – excuse me, but have you admitted a little girl lately? Her name is Ariel and she is my daughter." He slid the picture across the divider. The attendant picked it up and smiled. That was an encouraging sign for Gerald. Maybe they had admitted her while they were in the chapel. The attendant said, "She is adorable. My little sister's name is Ariel too. I am sorry, we haven't had anyone admitted in the last hour." His heart sank. The attendant slid the picture back to him. He stood still staring at the little girl in the picture for a long time. "Thank you for checking." He tried to take a step towards the sliding emergency entrance doors, but his legs weren't working, it was as if they were anchored to the floor and didn't want him to leave. There was a TV playing in the emergency room lobby. The reporter was giving reports of the tornado and the damage that it had caused. She remarked that based on the strength of the tornado, it was a miracle that there had been no loss of life reported thus far. She also said reports were still coming in. Since his legs didn't want to move, he turned back to the attendant. "Do you have a phone I could use?" The attendant handed him the phone. "Sorry, I need a phone book too, do you have one?" The attendant laughed. "Man, I haven't seen one of those since I visited my grandmother's house in Borger! Do they even make them anymore?" The attendant was having a good laugh at Gerald's expense. He quickly realized that Gerald wasn't in the mood for laughter and his expressions went soft. "Uh, who are you trying to call? I can look them up on my phone, it's pretty handy when it comes to that stuff." Gerald finally got his legs to move just a little and took a step back from the window. "I would like to call that reporter to let her know that my daughter is still missing." The attendant realized even more so that he should not have cracked the phone book joke. "Uh, yeah – I think she is channel 4. Here it is!" He dialed the number and asked for the reporter.

To his surprise, they put him through to her and she actually answered, leaving him completely off-guard. He was expecting to leave a message. "Uh, hey, we just saw your report about the tornado. Oh, yeah, I'm sorry, my name is Tommy and I work at Northwest Medical. Anyway, I am standing with a gentleman that would like to speak to you about his daughter; hang on, here he is." The attendant seemed a little rattled at having actually talked to a celebrity. "Hey – uh, Mr. Uh, here she is!" Gerald took the phone. "Yes, ma'am, my daughter was taken from my arms by that tornado and we haven't been able to find her. I was wondering if you could help me. I would be happy to pay you something to put it out there if needed. My wife won't talk to me anymore and I am at the end of my rope, ma'am." What he couldn't see was that she was scribbling notes. "Mr., uh, I am sorry I didn't catch your name." He looked around the emergency room for answers or something. He wasn't sure what he was looking for, he just wanted someone to help him. "My daughter's name is Ariel, Ariel Patterson. My name is Gerald and my wife is Nancy. See, she..." He started to tell her the story of how she was ripped from his arms, but she cut him off. "Mr. Patterson, I will be at

Northwest in five minutes. I was on my way there when you called so please sit tight and I will try and help you if I can. Do you happen to have a picture of your daughter with you? I would like to get her picture out to the public. I am sure she is ok, we just need to get Amarillo to help us find her." Finally, he thought. Someone who was willing to help in an effective way. "I will be in the emergency room waiting area, ma'am."

Chapter 46

MICHELLE AND SCOTT TURNED towards the voice. The little girl was still intubated so they knew the voice didn't come from her. Dr. Washburn made his way around the back side of her bed facing the wall giving Michelle the other side. "How about some ice chips? That will help moisten your mouth and throat, but because of all the medication you are currently on, I don't want to risk giving you too much water. You've had quite a day. Do you know where you are?" Michelle clutched her forearm instead of her bandaged hand.

That was the hand that was now missing a pinky finger. She would find out soon enough. Life would be odd sometimes without her pinky and she might get a few awkward looks, but she would be able to function just fine without it. The lady on the bed looked up at her and tried to mouth some more words but she simply couldn't get them to come out. Michelle reached for the ice chips sitting next to her, took a little spoon from the tray, and dished some out. "Just open your mouth a little and let these chips melt inside your mouth." She put the spoon on her lips and Renee did as she was instructed. It felt amazing to her. She had never been so thirsty in her whole life. She felt invigorated. It was only seconds before the first heap of chips were dissolved in her mouth.

Michelle scooped some more ice chips from the pitcher and repeated the steps. Each time Renee felt strength returning to her body. This was helping but what she really wanted was to guzzle a swimming pool full of water. "Let's take it nice and slow. We aren't in any hurry and you aren't going anywhere for a while." Although this woman appeared to be roughly the same age as Michelle, she placed her hand on the woman's forehead in a motherly way. There was that power of the human touch again. "Can you tell me your name?" Renee moved her tongue around her mouth to make sure it wasn't the gob of cotton balls she felt like it was just a minute ago, then she licked her lips.

It came out as a whisper, but it came out very clear. "Are you a collector?" Michelle looked at Scott, she was confused with the question. "No, honey, I am Dr. Michelle Hundlee and this is Dr. Scott Washburn. We've been in charge of your care since you came in. Can you tell me your name?" Dr. Washburn pulled his penlight from his pocket and leaned over Renee. "It's Renee." Michelle pulled her hand back from her forehead and placed it back on her bare forearm so Renee could feel that human touch.

"Ok, Renee, Dr. Washburn is going to ask you some questions and I want you to do what he says so we can help you get better, ok?" Renee nodded her head and seemed to relax, but Michelle seemed to see genuine fear in her eyes. "Look straight up at the ceiling, now follow my finger." Renee did as Dr. Washburn instructed and seemed to pass his tests. He shined his light directly into her eyes, which bothered her for a minute. "Do you know what happened to you?" Renee looked back up at the ceiling trying desperately to remember what happened, but her mind was stuck in the mud. She could not grind out a memory except the one of that creepy thing that was on top of her car. Michelle rubbed her forearm all the way up to Renee's shoulder. "It's ok, honey, we have you on just a smidge of morphine to help block out the pain. We are going to slowly move you off that and onto 800 milligrams of ibuprofen. Your head will clear up faster but unfortunately you will start to feel some of the pain from your burns. Fortunately for you, here at the VA, we are very good at fixing the burns." Renee nodded her head in acceptance and closed her eyes. Her eyes popped open just as quickly as they closed. The VA? What the hell was she doing at the VA? She wasn't a veteran and had no idea why she would be at the VA hospital. She tried to raise her left arm to get the doctor's attention, but it was too painful, so she whispered as loudly as she could. "Why am I at the VA?

What happened to me?" That was all she could get out, but it was enough to get Michelle's attention. "We don't know for sure exactly what happened to you, but a neighbor found you on your garage floor. You had burns all along the left side of your body. We are pretty certain that you took a pretty serious jolt of electricity that appears to have entered your hand and exited through your elbow. That's why you have the pain in your left arm. The bones that make up the joint were pretty fried, but we cleaned them out, reconstructed the nerve damage, and sewed you up. You're going to have trouble using that arm for a very long time. You will need therapy to help you regain the movement. Unfortunately, we were not able to save the little finger. That's why your hand is bandaged so heavily. It will be very tender and there will be some things that you can't do without a little finger, but I would say very little." Renee lifted her head to look down at her hand. It was weird, she felt like her pinky was there. She even felt like she was moving it at that very moment. "Electrocuted?" Renee needed some water and she was sure she would be able to speak more clearly but her throat still hurt really badly. "That's what it looks like. Do you remember anything about how it may have happened?" Renee shook her head, she did not remember, just the collector. "Water?" Michelle grabbed the pitcher of ice chips that had now melted into a mix of water and slush. "Ok, let's try and take a sip. I will hold your head up and you see how this feels. If there is any pain in your throat, let me know and we will get some fresh ice chips." Michelle held Renee's head up enough to allow her the ability to take a sip of the slush. It felt so good going down, but she could only handle a little bit. The doctor was right, her throat still hurt, and swallowing was not easy. "Ok, I think that's enough for now. I am going to go get some more ice chips and I will be right back."

Chapter 47

MARK MADE HIS WAY a little closer to where Annemarie was talking to the biker. Olivia was right on his arm with every step he took towards the general. He could see Wally staring at him and Wally motioned with his eyes to move to her right so that they would be directly behind Annemarie and the colonel. Mark complied, and they ended up about ten feet from where Annemarie was still sitting on the bunk beside the biker. "Lance Corporal, can you tell me what your objective was today? What was the cargo, where were you headed, and most importantly, who was the buyer?" Jack was still woozy, and he felt like he had kind of a hangover. "Why does a 4-star General want to know about a two-bit biker's cargo?" Annemarie got up from the bunk and grabbed a chair that was parked against the wall.

She slid the chair close to his bunk and sat down. She leaned forward with her elbows on her knees so she could move her face closer to his. "Lance Corporal, I ask the questions and you answer them. See, that's how it works. I asked them to remove your restraints out of respect for your service, show of good faith you might say. So just to show you that I am willing to give as much as I get, granted you play along, I will answer your question. I have been given orders to recover your cargo and return it to its rightful owner, which at this stage is the United States government." Jack shook his head as he was more confused than ever and thought he had been hearing things. "Why is Uncle Sam in the drug trade?" Annemarie looked around the room and smiled. She had this frustrated look to her, but it was comical to watch.

Mark knew this was a game and he enjoyed watching her play it. "See, there you go again, you clearly are taking more than you are giving. I am a patient woman, but I am about to reach my limit. Once again, I will accommodate your taking but this is where I balance the scales in my favor. Are we clear, Lance Corporal Ingle?" The biker seemed to respond to her military tactics quite well. "So, to answer your question, Uncle Sam is not in the drug running business. We are in the business of protecting citizens, which is what we are doing today. Now, tell me all about how we got to this point." Jack kicked his legs over the side of the bed and ended up directly face-to-face with the general. This caused a little stir in the room.

Mark was amazed at how Wally just seemed to appear in between Annemarie and the biker with his left hand tightly wrapped around the guys throat and pistol stuck directly between the eyes of the man. "Ease up, motherfucker, and get that gun out of my face. I was just moving my legs to make sure they work. I am not as stupid as you look. One move on that pretty General and every one of you pricks will deposit a bullet in me. I ain't fuckin' crazy either. Let me go so I can answer the bitch's question." Wally tensed up even more when he heard him call Annemarie a bitch again. "Respect for rank, Lance Corporal, or I'll be the only one to deposit a bullet in your ugly mug." Annemarie put her hand on Wally's back. "Ease up, Sergeant Major. I got this." Wally let go of his grip and he was out of sight as quickly as he had appeared. Mark still found this incredible. The man was some kind of Marine ninja. "Ok, boss, set this deal up. It was a huge payday; millions. This is money we have never seen before. These cats are Indian or Egyptian or something, I really don't know. We never met them. We have only talked to them on the phone. The one cat we speak to regularly, name is Omar, or at least that is what he tells us. He always seems mad at something. He is very difficult to talk to and I can't handle people like that, so Boss talked to the cocksucker so I wouldn't have to. Omar arranged a pick-up in Dallas and we were taking it to Los Angeles. We were supposed to drop it off at some dock where a couple of longshoremen were to take over from there. I didn't give a fuck what happened to the dope after that, I just knew that was one big ass payday. We were passing through Amarillo on I-40 when all hell broke loose and that's when me and Boss got separated under that underpass. The wind was blowing so hard and we were getting pelted with all kinds of shit. I couldn't keep my eyes open. We were locked arm-in-arm so we would hang on to each other, but when the wind stopped and it got quiet, I realized that Paul was gone – that's the one we call Boss. I didn't even feel him leave me. I don't know what the fuck happened to him, he was just gone. His bike was gone too. That was the craziest thing too; all our bikes were spared but his. We were looking for him when your scuba dudes showed up and started popping us with those dart guns. That's what I know and that is all I know." Annemarie looked at Mark and he could tell she believed the guy. He had no idea what his cargo was "How do you know it was drugs?" Jack's brow tightened as he thought through it. "I just assumed I guess. It was in these hard, yellow steel cases. There were four cases and it looked to me like there was no way to open them, kind of like they were welded shut or something. I didn't give a shit if they were super glued and I didn't give a shit if the camel jockeys wanted to get high. We just wanted the payday. They already slid us 900K before they even got the shit. I don't judge, I just ride." Annemarie leaned forward again, only this time she was more serious than ever. "Are you sure there were just four cases?" Without hesitation he replied, "Hell, yes, I am sure. You think one of us is skimming?"Annemarie shook her head no. "I don't believe that at all, I believe you had two cases, so I am to assume that Boss had the other two?" You could tell that the biker was starting to put some pieces of the puzzle together but not all of them. "Hell, yes, Boss had the other two. We aren't talking about drugs, are we? It was a shit ton more right?" Annemarie looked at Mark and smiled. She then turned her attention back to Jack. "A shit ton more than drugs, yes. You are lucky to be alive, Lance Corporal."

Annemarie stood up and pushed the chair back to where she found it. "What we need from you now is the address of where you were to deliver the cargo, any descriptions of the people you were to meet, names, numbers emails, that kind of thing. After you have given all the information to the Colonel here, you and your friends will be sent back to where you were first contacted. From there, I suggest that you spend the 900K you already have wisely and consider it severance. If you are contacted in any way other than the methods we are already tracking you with – and believe me, we know every-thing about you, families, mistresses, and all your illegal and legal activities – we will pick you up again and only this time, you will never be heard from again. Trust me, Lance Corporal Ingle, if you pick up a cheap ass burner phone from your local Walmart or 7-11, we will know. In other words, don't fuck with me." Mark got a chill down his spine when he heard the woman he fantasized about be such a brute. There was nothing sexy about that. Maybe he should move on from this particular fantasy. Nope, not even her brutish, chilling behav-ior could sway him.

Annemarie turned to the mad scientist. "Please have the cargo secured properly, encased as instructed, and placed aboard our aircraft. We will be leaving for Atlanta in thirty minutes. Ms. Millben, please go with the doctor to supervise the encasement to CDC standards. I want to get to Texas ASAP to find the other boxes." The mad scientist looked a little confused when she told him to get the cargo ready. "General, the Colonel has already secured the cargo." Mark had always believed he had a knack for spotting trouble and being prepared for it; this was trouble.

Annemarie turned to the colonel while aiming her comments at the mad scientist. "The cargo is not the Colonel's to secure." She turned directly to the colonel now. "Colonel, is there some sort of deficiency in your hearing and comprehension of orders?" Mark took a survey of his surroundings for some reason. Maybe it was his instincts. Perhaps he was looking for the nearest exit, but in truth, his mind was telling him to count the number of people in the room and exactly where they were standing. He had a wall behind him so there was no one that could be behind him. row of shelves was to his left that blocked some of the line of sight of the rest of the room, but for some tactical reason that he couldn't quite explain to himself, he felt like he and Olivia were in a pretty good spot. "General, my hearing is just fine. My comprehension skills are exceptional, better than yours actually. The way I comprehend the situation is that I have what you and the President don't want the rest of the world to have, and I am in a good position to negotiate its safe return to the US government, thus keeping it out of the hands of people that may use it not for the good of man, but for ill-gotten purposes." Mark hated that guy. He was smug and smarmy and everything about him screamed arrogant schoolyard bully.

Annemarie never took her eyes off the colonel and even took a step closer to him. The air in the room was being sucked up by the presence of these two soldiers that were now locked in a very deadly game of cat and mouse. "Colonel, you say your comprehensions skills are better than mine? That's debatable but for the sake of argument I will concede for now. The real comprehension skills come when someone is under duress. You know how a buck private on the battlefield is suddenly thrust into command of his unit when his NCO is killed? And for some unexplainable reason, without any leadership train-ing, they make all the right decisions and become heroes, or in some cases, they curl up in the fetal position and pray for a quick death." The colonel cracked a smile; Mark thought it was a sinister one. "General, I've seen lots of combat, way more than you. I should have been wearing your stars. If it weren't for the military becoming some experimental petri dish for societal changes – where if a woman can manage to pass through West Point, learn to salute, and play a political game – she gets moved ahead of hard working battle tested soldiers. Oh, I comprehend things way better than you, no debate there." Annemarie rubbed her chin as if she was digesting all his BS. Mark felt his butt clench very tight, it always happened when he was nervous. Sometimes he would clinch it so tight that it would sort of twitch. He had no way of controlling it and only hoped that his ass wouldn't start twitching now and make noise. "I wasn't speaking of you, Colonel. I know your service record very well; you are a very brave combat Commander and there is no doubt. I was referring to your second." The colonel looked around the room but didn't respond; he just kept that sinister smile on his face. Annemarie continued, "You see, seconds are strange creatures sometimes. Sometimes a second is a second for a reason. You see, they love the thrill of being saluted and sort of having the emperor's ear if you will, but when it comes down to actual leadership, they too end up in the fetal position. Do you play an instrument, Colonel, piano or strings or maybe even a guitar?" Mark heard that and his butt started twitching. Was she warning him that the code words were coming? Holy cow, his mind went into hyper drive.

He could see that Olivia caught it too and he noticed her eyelid was twitching. Maybe her nerves got to her too and instead of her ass going ape shit, it was her eyelids. Apparently, Annemarie and Wally had their own code words worked out because before the colonel could answer the musical quiz, a bullet went through one side of his head and out the other. He dropped right where he stood. No dramatic hurling across the room with the force of the bullet, it was just like he dropped straight down in kind of a kneeling position and slumped over. That was the end of the smarmy colonel.

Mark heard all kinds of sounds at that moment. First, the sound of the gun going off in this room was still echoing in his ears. Second, the sight of a man dropping to the ground was not easy to stomach. Wally had skillfully placed himself in a position that was quite tactical. He placed himself where if anyone shot at him, he had ample cover and Annemarie could also make a relatively quick exit. Mark understood now why Wally had positioned he and Olivia earlier when he guided them to this spot with his eyes.

He thought Annemarie would move out of the center of the room, but she never budged, not an inch. "Gentlemen, I want my bug and I am willing to die right here in this God-forsaken place in defense of my country. I am waiting to find out if the late colonel's second in command would like to step up and effectively lead his men or perhaps would like to assume the fetal position. It is the moment of truth, gentlemen. DOD knows we are here and all those double doors you and I went through are now locked down and are in firm control of the Pentagon. My orders are to bring that shit back to Atlanta or die with all of you right here. Either way, those boxes of mass death are worthless to you and you will never leave this bunker." She was screaming at the top of her lungs and Mark felt like there was not one ounce of drama in the pitch. She meant it and his ass was twitching out of control.

Chapter 48

JAKE USED HIS BIG TREE TRUNK looking legs to push the almost rotted fence post over. It wasn't very hard actually. The rancher would need to replace those anyway, Jake thought. Paul took a minute to rest. Ariel was still in his arms but wasn't saying much. Her breathing seemed to improve but what did he know? He was guessing. He knew his own breathing was not improving and his chest still hurt like hell. Jake stood and looked over the horizon, it seemed so vast to him. He couldn't believe that Texas had this much land. How in the hell did these three ever get so far away from civilization? "You ok, man? You wanna stop to rest a bit?" Paul shook his head no. He simply wanted to get the hell back to Renee. He has never in his life wanted anything more than that. "No, let's get going. No telling how many more fences we have to knock down to get out of this God-forsaken country." Jake laughed. "Dude, don't you know this is God's country? He hasn't forsaken it. He just rationed the water for it." Ariel lifted her head ever so slightly. "You shouldn't say that. My daddy says it's bad. My daddy needs me to help him. When will we get back?" It came out as a whisper but both Jake and Paul heard it clearly. She was very weak but was ok at least. She laid her head back down on Paul's shoulder. "A bee stung me." She muttered against Paul's neck. Paul moved her towards him so he could see her face. "Where did a bee sting you, kid? Show me." He was confused because he felt like if a bee had stung her she would have at least kicked up a fuss or cried or something, but she had been asleep the whole time. Her eyes were closed and her head was bobbing around like one of those dogs you see on a car dashboard sometimes.

Jake came over to help look to see if he could see any swelling or a mark of any kind but found nothing. "She has to be dreaming. We would have heard her if she was stung." Paul put her head back on his shoulder. Jake climbed back on the bike and kicked it to life. Paul gingerly slung his legs over the back of the bike with Ariel in between them again. As soon as they were rolling again, Paul began to dream about getting back to Renee. He knew she would marry him. Of that he had no doubt. He wondered what she was doing right now. She was probably worried about him because he should have contacted her by now. They were always texting or talking. She made his life more organized and she made it more peaceful.

He could feel that Jake was moving a little faster than normal and he also noticed that the terrain was quite a bit smoother.

"I see the loop man! We will be on pavement in just a few minutes!" Even with the roar of the Panhead, Paul heard that. Paul glanced around Jake's shoulder to see for himself and sure enough, there was a road. What seemed like only seconds to Paul, they were at the road's edge. No more fences to knock down, just open road. Maybe he had passed out for a few minutes again. Maybe Jake had already knocked down the fence. He had no idea, but he didn't care. All he could think about was getting back to Renee and finding this little girl's parents. "Make sure you hang on, man, we have the open road and I am dropping the hammer." Paul nodded and patted Jake's shoulder in approval.

Paul was expecting a blast of wind with the acceleration, but he got nothing. He could see the road moving quickly below them but there was no wind, no noise other than the hum of the Panhead. He had no idea how long they had been on the road before he saw the road beneath them slow down until finally it stopped moving at all. Paul couldn't lift his head upright. He felt like he was as weak as he had ever been in his life. He struggled to hang on to Ariel. "Where you fellas headed?" Paul could hear a different voice and it gave him a little life. An actual person! That meant that they were getting close. Paul lifted his head to see a very old man standing beside the road. "Mister, where's your car? Why are you out here in the middle of nowhere, did your car break down someplace?" Jake seemed as confused as Paul. He dropped the kickstand

and let the bike rest. "Oh, I don't live far from here. This is how I stay young. I like to walk. I can't run anymore but I keep moving. Might not be able to tell but I was quite a runner in my day. I had a scholarship in track and then December 7th, 1941 happened. I got so upset, like every other able-bodied kid at that time, I couldn't wait to sign up and exact some revenge. Where you headed?" Jake was now standing in front of the old guy.

Paul thought that next to Jake, the old guy seemed so small and so frail. He was nuts for being out here walking on the side of the road. He could have a heart attack and keel over. The buzzards would pick him clean before anyone found him. "We are headed to Amarillo. We got caught up in the tornado and need to get some medical help. You wouldn't happen to have a phone, would you?" The old man lifted his ball cap and rubbed his forehead then placed the cap back on his head. "No, sir, never had one. I got one at home, but it was disconnected years ago. I enjoy the peace and quiet. If you are headed to Amarillo, I heard the main hospital got overrun and started sending folks to the VA. You might want to go there. The girl's parents will probably be there soon." Paul thought that was a weird piece of advice from a guy on foot in the middle of the Panhandle without a cell phone. How the hell did he know she wasn't the daughter of Jake or himself? "Thanks, mister. We need to get moving. I would offer you a ride, but you can see we are out of room." The old guy laughed. "Son, I don't need a ride. I always get where I am going, and I am never in a hurry. Say 'hello' to the folks at the VA." With that, the old guy patted Jake on the shoulder and lifted his cap again to brush the hair back on his head. He placed the cap back on his head. Paul noticed the writing on the cap and thought that was a weird name for a ship. What the hell is a Batfish?

Chapter 49

GERALD HANDED THE PHONE back to the attendant. "I'm just going to sit over here in the waiting room. I shouldn't say this, but I am tired of the chapel." The attendant smiled at Gerald and went back to typing. Even though the room was still crowded, it had calmed down quite a bit. Most of the people in the room now were friends and relatives of those who were being treated. Everyone in the room kept their voices down to a whisper. Gerald found a little comfort in the whispers. He liked that everyone had respect for each other's space, physical and mental. Even though he was a farmer he loved to people watch. He loved to imagine what they were thinking and tried to place them on their respective genealogy trees, where they were born, what continent their roots originated, and how they judged him.

He was people watching a middle-aged woman who was dressed to the nines. She seemed out of place not only in this waiting room, but to Gerald, she seemed out of place for

West Texas. He imagined her in Dallas more than Amarillo. He thought she was probably a Dallas socialite. Maybe her private jet couldn't take off in the storm, who knows? He just knew she didn't belong in this situation. "That storm was really something, wasn't it? We haven't seen a storm like that in 50 years." Gerald heard the words, but he wasn't sure if they were meant for him. He looked to his left and no one was there. He looked to his right and he was staring directly into the face of an older man. He didn't know how old, but it was pretty old in his book. His ears were big, and his nose was big. He always heard that when you got older, your face shrinks or your ears and nose just get bigger. This man was staring directly at Gerald. "Yes." Was all Gerald could get out. He didn't want to chit-chat with anyone. He was not in any mood for conversation, especially with an old fart. "I've seen a lot of crazy things in my day but nothing like that. I actually watched that cloud turn gray and start swirling around. It was so peaceful at first, you know, like the heavens were just playing around, and then all the sudden, the cloud acted like it got angry. Reminded me of a kid I went to school with back in Kirpatrick Elementary School when I was just a snot-nosed kid, I believe it would have had to have been around 1932. He was a nice kid most of the time but when he got mad he took on the most awful disposition you could ever know. He would knock the girls down, give the boys a knuckle sandwich, and most of the time, nobody knew why. And later, he would act as if nothing happened. It was like he had no memory of being such a bruiser. Barganonni, I believe was his name. I found out later he got killed on a PT boat when it rammed into a Japanese submarine. He was the skipper of that boat and if I had to make a guess, he got mad, had one of his fits, and decided to just take his little boat and ram that submarine out of spite. You never know. Nobody knows how a PT boat managed to get tangled up with a sub anyway. He must have caught them ventilating. Yes, sir, he sure had a temper." Gerald started to get up to get away from this fossil but something inside was telling him to be polite. He needed to at least let the man know he wasn't in the mood to chat. Just as he was about to speak the old man started again. "Those submarines were scary. I hated the water but my whole class back in 42 decided to join the Navy. We were all Texans, West Texans at that, hadn't seen much of any water and word had it that the Navy boys got all the girls. Now that wasn't the reason we went in. We all wanted to get back at the Japanese for sure, but we figured if we were going to go exact some revenge, we might as well pick up some girls on the way. I ended up on a doggone submarine. The most scared I've ever been in my life was on that thing. We were being hunted in the South Pacific, we were spotted ventilating ourselves and had to quickly dive to try and hide. That cruiser started dropping depth charges like crazy. We could actually hear them splash when they hit the water and all you could do was wait. Every time those charges would explode, our sub would nearly roll over. I sure didn't want to drown. The captain outsmarted them, and we not only ended up poking a hole in their hull with one of our torpedoes, we also managed to pick up a German U boat nearby and nailed that little bastard too. Weird thing when you hear a boat explode under water. You can almost hear their crew screaming and drowning. Terrible way to die I reckon."

Gerald pretended like he was interested as best he could, but he was in no mood to listen. "First off, thank you for your service to our country but..." Gerald was trying to tell the old guy he wasn't in the mood when the old man interrupted again. Gerald thought maybe the old man was deaf, but he heard the next words very clearly. "I lost a child once, nearly tore me and my wife apart at the time. I'd come home from the war, was tired of seeing death, and was ready to settle down. It turned out that it wasn't true that the sailors got all the girls because I never once even winked at a girl in the four years I was in the Navy. Anyway, as luck would have it, I met her in a church in San Diego. She was the most beautiful woman I'd ever seen. I knew the minute I saw her that if I couldn't have her, there would be no other because no other compared. It took a while, but she wised up and married me. I think it took a while because her dad just hated me. He was a senator from California and was expecting her to marry way better than me, but I just didn't care. Anyway, we bought a ranch here in Amarillo, settled down, and had as many kids as she let me. I wanted a bunch, you see. We ended up having eight kids in all, six girls and two boys. Twin girls were the last of the bunch. Boy that was a shocker. Back then they didn't know if you were having twins, they just kept yankin' 'em out if needed. I was so excited. I couldn't believe my good fortune. God gave me two girls at once! We named them Ariel and Amy."

Gerald was listening now. "You have a daughter named Ariel?" The old man put his head down and looked at his hands, they were big hands, seen a lot of work hands. Even as old as this man looked, Gerald was impressed by the strength in his hands. He hadn't noticed until now. "Had, I'm afraid." Gerald could see the old guy getting choked up. "It's been over 50 years ago and still hurts today like it did that day." He raised his head back up and clasped his hands together as if he was about to pray but he just intertwined his fingers together to help him steady himself. "What happened to her, if you don't mind I ask?" The old guy just shook his head as if to say he didn't mind. "I wish I knew. Her and her sister liked to run down to the mailbox and check the mail. It was quite a way away from the house so it was sort of like an adventure for them. They would take off lickidy split at 3:00 p.m. every day to bring back the mail. One day, Amy came back and Ariel didn't. Amy was beat up pretty bad and couldn't say a word. We tried and tried to get her to tell us what happened, just give us some idea of how to find her sister, but she couldn't. She never was the same. She lost her childhood and her sister that day. I've hunted for her sister every day of my wore-out life. I expect I am getting down to the point where I get to see her again in heaven and I get to ask her to forgive me for not being strong enough to protect her. My wife couldn't handle it at all. She faked it for a few years after that, but she wasn't foolin' me. I knew her too well. She felt the guilt just like I did but it was just too much for her to handle. She took a hand full of pills one night before she went to sleep and never woke up. She did it that way so I wouldn't think anything of it. She went to bed every night after me. She snored so loud that we had worked out a system that I went to sleep first and then she would come to bed a few minutes after me. She took the pills, threw the empty bottle in the trash, and went to bed. I was snuggled up to her most of the night like I usually did but somewhere around 4:00 a.m. I got cold and realized she was so cold. I knew it before I turned on the light that she was gone. I cried like a baby. I don't know if it's actually true or not but if the good book is right, I won't get to see her when I see Ariel. They don't let quitters into heaven. I can't say I blame her. I can't tell you how many times I've had the barrel of a gun in my mouth or stuck to the side of my head only to realize that I ain't no quitter. It just never occurred to me that she might just quit." The tears freely ran down his face as he recounted the day that his daughter went missing.

Gerald could see his own pain in this man's face. "My daughter is missing too but I know it's definitely my fault that she is missing." Gerald felt the emotions coming up in him again and fought it back. He didn't want to be blubbering tears when that reporter got here. "How's it your fault?" Gerald thought about the best way to tell the Reader's Digest version of the story and decided on "the tornado ripped her from my arms." The old man unclasped his fingers and put his hand on Gerald's knee.

Gerald felt a calm come over him like he had never felt before. "So, you are stronger than God, you are stronger than the powerful forces of God's nature. You must be one tough kid." He had a slight chuckle mixed with a snivel from clearing up the tears. "No, I am not, but a man ought to be able to protect his daughter." Gerald caught himself as he said it and knew he was talking to someone who needed no more reminders of a father's responsibility. "I'm sorry, I didn't mean anything by that." The old man smiled. "It's ok, son. I understand." The old guy slowly rose to his feet and used Gerald's shoulder to help him steady himself. He looked around and found his cane. Once he had stabled himself, he stood straight as an arrow; Gerald thought it was impressively straight. He calculated during the conversation that the man was probably on the other side of 90 years old. The old guy stuck out his worn but strong hand. "Son, the Lord never gives you more than you can bear. I know what you are thinking right now, and I understand, but I hope you decide to keep that pistol tucked into the back of your pants. It won't solve anything, only makes it worse. I'm sure Ariel will show up very soon.

In fact, I guarantee it." Gerald couldn't hold back the tears at hearing the old man's declaration. He looked up at him standing before him. The old man pulled his cap off and ran his fingers through his hair and placed the cap back on his head. Gerald could see the cap clearly. He could read the top of the cap and thought it was odd, he's never heard of the USS Batfish.

The old man patted Gerald on the shoulder and said his good-bye. With that, he walked out the emergency room door and he was gone. Once the doors slid shut and Gerald could no longer see him, he recounted what the old guy said; he guaranteed Ariel would show up. Was he talking about his Ariel or my Ariel? Wait a damn minute, he thought, I never told him my daughter's name. He got up and ran out the sliding doors smack into the reporter he was waiting for, sending her sprawling on the sidewalk.

Chapter 50

AFTER THE SMARMY COLONEL went down and Annemarie staked her flag in the ground with her declaration of war, the room remained quiet for a second and then a strong voice came from the left of where Mark was standing. Mark looked around but couldn't pinpoint the location. He looked at Annemarie and she was still standing firm. He could not see where Wally was though. He had obviously changed his position. His mind raced, what happens if he actually had to shoot someone? He didn't think he could do it. His stomach starting churning and his ass twitching was now out of control. He felt Olivia touch his arm which actually helped him. There was that power of the human touch again.

The power of her touch didn't last long; all hell broke loose after that. I guess the colonel's men decided they were in too deep and began shooting. Mark instinctively pushed Olivia to the ground, where he then flopped on top of her to shield her. Fight or flight, huh? That was a bunch of horseshit. He was scared to death and if he could run he would have. Hell, there was nowhere to run, all the doors behind them were locked so there was no retreat from Long Island for him. He raised his head just enough to look around but could no longer see Annemarie. He figured she had to be ok because the firing was intense. He figured that meant that Wally was still shooting and hopefully Annemarie was too.

He reached down towards his hip for the gun they had given him. He tried to remember all the instructions on how to shoot the damn thing. He pulled the gun from the holster and raised it up to eye level. He had to turn over on his back in order to figure out the steps for shooting. He remembered the safety feature and, oh yeah, you had push and pull in order to get the bullet in the barrel or something like that. The noise was deafening in this place. He finally caught a glimpse of Wally moving behind a row of shelves. They made eye contact at that moment. Wally made the motion for Mark to look behind him. Mark thought it was weird that Wally seemed to be enjoying this. He was actually smiling.

Mark turned to look in the direction that Wally had motioned and could see that two other soldiers, obviously the colonel's men, were kneeling and firing in their direction, but he and Olivia were too low to the floor for them to get a good shot. Holy shit, they were trying to kill him! Just then he saw both of them drop in a heap just like the colonel. Wally had circled behind them and put two bullets in their heads in rapid succession. Boy this was real, he thought. He looked for Wally to offer thanks, but he was gone again. He had no idea where to look now. He put his head back down and snuggled up against Olivia who surprisingly seemed very calm. He tried to whisper in her ear over the noise of gunshots. "How many men do you remember seeing?" She didn't know and made the motion to back up that lack of knowledge.

He looked towards where he thought Annemarie should be and could see a boot sticking out from behind a computer desk. Judging by the small size of the boot it had to be her. It was moving so she was still ok. He felt a tap on his leg and spun around with the gun extended. Wally slowly pushed the gun back down and smiled. "Wrong enemy, Sir, shooting me will only make your day worse. It pisses me off and you don't want to see me pissed." Mark could not believe that this guy showed comedic talent at a moment like this, hell, maybe he wasn't joking. Maybe Wally was one of those robot soldiers. "See that door to your 6? Start making your way there. You won't run into me for a few minutes so if you cross paths with anyone in uniform, kill 'em." With that, Wally was on the move again.

Six? What the hell did that mean my six? Oh! It hit him. The clock thing! 12 is straight and 6 is behind you. He tapped Olivia on the back, but it turned out to be her butt. *Geez – I* hope she doesn't sue me for sexual harassment, he thought. He didn't mean to touch her butt, although she did have a nice butt. She made eye contact and he couldn't read any sexual harassment in her body language, so he felt like he was safe. The sounds of all these guns going off at the same time made it hard to hear and everything seemed muffled at the time, so he motioned for her to follow him. He managed to spin around, and she did the same. They started crawling towards the door that Wally had pointed out. They made it to the door, but it was shut as Annemarie had already pointed out to everyone.

As Mark was trying to understand why he had been pointed to a closed door, Wally showed up again. "I know where they all are now, so does Annemarie. This will be over in just a second; just stay here by the door. It's the safest place." As Wally was unveiling the grand plan to Mark, Mark saw a uniformed figure approach directly from behind Wally. He could easily see that it wasn't Annemarie, which meant that this guy was on the other team. For some unknown reason that Mark would not be able to explain later, he raised his gun and pulled the trigger. He didn't take aim, he just pointed the gun in the direction of the other guy. This startled Wally and for the first time ever, Mark saw something other than confidence and calm on his face, he saw the face of confusion.

Obviously, Wally had miscalculated and did not know where they all were, or he would not have allowed this bozo to get behind them. The bullet struck the man directly in the knee cap area. Mark thought it was a good shot for not ever shooting a pistol, but obviously this was a bad shot in a combat zone because the other guy wasn't dead and could still pull a trigger, which he did. Wally spun around and fired three shots which all struck the man in the face. Mark's first thought was that at least his knee cap wouldn't hurt anymore, but then he felt a warm sensation running down his arm, back, and shoulder. Olivia saw it first and without hesitation, pulled Mark from a sitting position to lying flat on his back. Wally threw something at her and he was off roaming the barracks again.

Mark felt kind of dizzy and thought for a second that he might throw up, but he fought it back down. He was a bit confused because Olivia was all over him, her hands were up around his neck, which seemed like she was trying to snuggle. Maybe she liked being patted on the ass. Mark was sure that he must have tripped her trigger. He needed to stop her and let her know that although she was very attractive, there was only one woman for him and she was somewhere in this room. Besides, Olivia was just too young for him. It wouldn't look right. He was about to break her heart when the gunfire suddenly stopped. It was quiet again. He started to sit up, but Olivia pushed him back down. "I have to stop the bleeding. Be still." Mark thought to himself, what bleeding? That guy has three bullets in his face and one in his knee, he's beyond repair. Olivia could see the confusion in his eyes and whispered, "You're bleeding, don't make it worse by squirming." He could feel the internal panic rising for sure now. Oh, hell, here comes that ass twitching. If my ass starts twitching out of control it could force me to bleed out, what the hell?! He didn't even remember getting shot. Maybe that direct hit to the knee he delivered to the bad guy was just his imagination, maybe when he raised his gun to shoot he had actually shot himself!

Oh, how embarrassing that would be back at the White House. He could see the headlines: White House Chief of Staff Mortally Wounded Himself in a Gunfight. That would be just awful. As he was thinking about all the new headlines that would make fun of this poor marksmanship, he heard her voice. "Sergeant Major! All clear here." Then he heard Wally return, "Copy that, ma'am. Perimeter secured!" He heard the shuffling of feet coming towards them and once again tried to sit up, but once again Olivia pushed him back down. "Lt. here saved my life and took one in the throat." Wally bent down and practically pushed Olivia out of the way. He removed the gauze that he had given her to cover the wound to inspect the damage. "Can you talk?" At first Mark wasn't sure that Wally was talking to him but decided he better answer anyway. "Yeah, I can talk." But it only came out as a whisper.

Wally threw the bloody gauze aside and applied a new one. This time he wrapped it all the way around Mark's neck to keep it there. Annemarie had positioned herself directly above Mark in his line of sight. Mark was disappointed that she wasn't kneeling over him, fawning over him, weeping for him to not die. Instead she stood over them scanning the room for other intruders. "Can he move?" Wally was still bandaging Mark's neck as he replied, "I've had worse cuts shaving with my field knife. He will be fine." Annemarie stepped out from where Mark could not see her but could still hear her. "All of the colonel's men are dead. Unfortunately, the bikers that were still comatose were used as shields and didn't fare so well. Unfortunately, Lance Corporal Ingle didn't make it. Deep down he was a good man and unfortunately all these men will never receive a proper funeral because the world will never know what happened to them. Where's that mad ass scientist? He knows where the bug is, and I want it." Wally found the mad scientist hiding under a bunk. "Ma'am, I have him right here." Wally reached under the bunk and yanked the man practically to his feet all in one motion.

Annemarie made her way over to the mad scientist. "Say, doc, you've had ringside seats to quite a show. In the business world I'd say you've reached an inflection point in your career. A point where you make some choices that can be dire in all regards. Where's my bug?" The mad scientist heard the same click that Mark heard, which was the distinct sound of a hammer being cocked on a gun. "I know it seems like an eternity ago for a scholarly man like you but try and think back just a few minutes; the colonel was at that same inflection point and he sure chose poorly. We really don't need you, you know. The bug is here on the compound. We will find it. It just takes more time and time is what I do not have. Wally!"

Her shouting Wally made everyone jump, including the mad scientist. He knew that meant she was giving Wally the green light to put a bullet in his head just like he had the colonel's. "Two doors back, left corridor in a room labeled Cold Storage." Wally put a bullet in his head anyway. "Dammit, Wally! You can't just execute a man like that! It's not right! He told you what you wanted to know!" Mark's throat hurt but he let out his frustrations of just having witnessed two executions. He slowly stood and faced Wally directly. "Lt., you're in over your head." Annemarie stepped directly in between the two men and pulled her SAT phone from her pocket. She hit one button and waited for a few seconds. "Yes, Sir, we have half the virus in our possession. All targets have been neutralized. Yes, Sir, the cargo is secured and will be in route to CDC Atlanta in fifteen minutes." She put the phone back in her jacket pocket. "Olivia, there is a plane waiting for you to escort the virus safely back to CDC. Your work is done here. I am certain you understand that any public disclosure of events you encountered here today will be dealt with swiftly." Olivia nodded in compliance as anyone would after witnessing such brutality. "Fuck that, Annemarie – she risked her life today and all you do is threaten her? She should get a medal for serving her country and doing the right thing and all she gets is fear! That's bullshit, and you know it!" Mark was livid.

Olivia put her hand on Mark in such a calm way. She moved close to him. She stood on her tiptoes and whispered in his ear. "I understood the rules before I left Atlanta. They made it clear to me. I have no regrets and you can pat my ass anytime you feel like it. Don't worry, secrets are safe with me." He looked down at her, he had never looked so deeply into any-one's eyes before. This kid was genuine, she was tougher than she looked and deserved better, but he knew she was right. Besides, he was off the hook for sexual harassment now and if things didn't work out for him and Annemarie, he would go look her up. She was cute as hell and he really didn't give a shit if she was so young. Things weren't looking too good between him and Annemarie at the moment. He was seeing a very cold and callous person that he didn't anticipate. How in the world could anyone as beautiful as Annemarie be that cold as to condone the execution of two men? Mark was really struggling with all this.

"The three of us are headed to West Texas to find the other vials." There was no debate in Annemarie's command. "Wheels up in 15, Wally, let's make it quick." Wally moved like a ghost and was off to retrieve the vials before Mark could say another word.

Chapter 51

DR. HUNDLEE AND DR. WASHBURN continued to make their rounds among the patients that had been so unexpectedly dropped into their care. After they left the room Renee was in along with the little girl, they continued down the hall room by room checking on each one. They were pleased with their work and discussed the possibility of transporting the more minor conditions to Northwest. They knew they couldn't risk moving the four at the end of the hallway directly across from the nurses' station. They made a U pattern in their room check and ended up across the hall from where they began with the electrocuted woman and the little girl. The staff had dubbed the little girl Ariel because of her mermaid underwear she was wearing when they brought her in. They had no idea they were dead-on accurate in their labeling.

Dr. Hundlee entered the room with the two men followed by Dr. Washburn. She screamed when she saw the big man standing over the man with the badly swollen face trying to smother him with a pillow. Dr. Washburn was a pretty big man himself and knocked Dr. Hundlee to the ground as he pushed his way past her. He was in a difficult spot because if he tackled the man, the force of the two men moving forward would land on top of the man with the swollen face and may send him back into cardiac arrest. He may be dead already, no telling how long he has had that pillow over his head, so he made the choice of trying to reach around the big man's neck and pull backwards. He got a nice grip around his neck and began to pull back. Dr. Hundlee was back on her feet and had entered the fray. She was pulling with Dr. Washburn and they managed to get the pillow off the patient's face.

The big man was hell-bent on killing this man because he resisted their grip by continuing to press forward toward the defenseless man in the bed. Everyone on the floor heard the commotion and began to pile into the room. Two orderlies jumped into the struggle, which was much needed. Dr. Washburn was out of breath and was about to lose his grip on this giant man. Between the two doctors and the two orderlies, they managed to push the man back onto his bed. Well, as best they could, he was half laying on the bed and half on the floor. The orderlies each had a leg and had pinned them to the floor leaving Michelle and Scott to wrestle with the man's giant arms and upper torso. This proved to be a challenge for both. "Nurse, we need 20 milligrams of Haloperidol STAT! I can't hold this guy much longer!" Dr. Washburn was breathing hard as he said it.

Everyone in the room was tense. You could hear the orderlies breathing hard, as was Dr. Hundlee. The big man never let up. Michelle thought he was one giant hunk of tense gristle. Why was this man so hell- bent on killing the patient next to him? Just as she was thinking that, the big man gave them somewhat of a clue. "He is a collector! Don't let him get to her!" The needle went into the man's right arm and the room got even more tense wondering if the drug would even work. Michelle was second- guessing whether or not 20mgs was enough to stop the hulk from his killing spree. What seemed like an eter- nity passed as they waited on the drugs calming effects to kick in, but in reality, it was about three minutes. The orderlies felt his legs loosen first, then Michelle could feel his arms relax.

Dr. Washburn never felt anything as his adrenalin was in high gear. He still had a firm grip on the patient and hadn't real- ized that he was the only one still holding the big man down. Michelle put her hand on his back; there was that power of the human touch again. "Dr. Washburn, you can let go now. He is sedated and relaxed." Beneath her hand she could feel the doctor exhale as he slid off the bed and all the way to the floor. He was now sitting on the floor against the big man's bed with his head leaned back and his eyes closed. "Geez, I am out of gas. I had no more energy left to hold him down. Give me a minute to catch my breath and I will be fine." He sat there perfectly still staring at the ceiling. One of the orderlies went outside and brought the doctor back a bottle of water.

Dr. Washburn took the bottle but couldn't twist off the cap; he just didn't have the strength.

The orderly quickly recognized the problem, grabbed the bottle back from the doctor, opened it and handed it back to him. Dr. Washburn took a sip and handed it back to the orderly who then took three huge gulps and handed it to the other orderly who then finished it off. When he realized he should have offered some to Michelle, he got embarrassed. "I'm sorry, ma'am, I can go get you another one. I was out of gas myself." Michelle smiled a quick smile and reassured him that she was fine. The orderlies then helped Dr. Washburn up off the floor then managed to push the big man's legs back up on to the bed. It soon hit Dr. Hundlee that no one had checked on the man with the swollen face. She practically leaped over to his bed. She felt his carotid artery and immediately found a pulse. She reached for her stethoscope, but it was not there. She looked around the room and saw it lying on the floor in the corner. The nurse saw it too and quickly stepped over to retrieve it and hand it back to her.

His heart rate was normal, and all his vitals were good. "Doctor, I think we should remove his tube. Maybe we should move him to another room in case he wakes up and tries to kill him again." She motioned to the big man now sedated in the bed across the room from this man. "That won't be necessary" came a voice with a serious Texas drawl. Everyone in the room turned to the big man in the bed that had just taken 20mgs of Haloperidol. Michelle tensed up, but in spite of her fears of another wrestling match, she made her way back across the room to the man's bedside.

Dr. Washburn had already positioned himself between the big man and the defenseless man in preparation for another tag team match. "Did I hurt him? I thought he was someone else. I can see now that he isn't what I thought he was. I was just a little out of my head for a second. Where am I?" Dr. Washburn grabbed the man's wrist and checked his heart rate. "Fascinating, hardly an increased heart rate. All the struggling and your heart has a superb rhythm." "Takes a little more than a wrestling match to get my heart going, Doc." Dr. Washburn let go of his wrist. "I see that. Look straight up at the ceiling. Follow my finger, please." The big man did as he was told. "What's your name?"

The big man's expression was comical as he felt like he had almost forgotten his own name. "Uh, I'm Jake Johannson. The tornado caught up to me, didn't it?" Dr. Washburn didn't respond but asked another question. "Who is President?" Jake thought about it for a second and said, "Barack

Hussein Obama." Everyone in the room smiled to see if he was joking but Jake never offered up a correction. "Well Mr. Johannson, you probably have a concussion. Yes, the tornado must have caught up with you because you were brought in by ambulance. We aren't sure of the details and hoped you could fill us in, but I can see that you still need a little more rest. Can you at least maybe help us understand why you were trying to kill this man next to you?"

Jake scratched his head and thought about it long and hard. He knew why but he wasn't sure if they would believe him if he told them about the collectors. He damn sure didn't want any white coats coming into the room and moving him to a padded cell somewhere. "I'm a Texas Ranger, Doc. I've seen some bad stuff in my day and I have some bad dreams every now and then. I thought this guy was someone I failed to catch a long time ago. If I told you some of the things that guy had done to some children up in the Hill Country, you'd all be lining up with pillows. That guy didn't have any tattoos though. That should have been a signal for me in my haze, but I missed it. I swear I hope I didn't hurt him. He looks pretty bad." Jake was proud of himself for his quick thinking. The story about the pervert in the Hill Country was true but they didn't need to know that. He never caught that murdering child molester, but they didn't need to know he thought that disfigured grotesque face across the room from him was one of those collectors he had killed earlier and had seen on the side of the road just after they left the old guy with the Batfish cap.

Chapter 52

GERALD TUMBLED TO THE GROUND, more in defense of not landing directly on the lady he had just sent sprawling on the sidewalk. He bent his pinky on his left hand back somehow when he landed on the sidewalk. The lady was in a skirt and it managed to hike up past her underwear. Gerald was very embarrassed to have knocked this poor lady to the ground, but he was more embarrassed to have glanced at the thong at a time when he had no business thinking of ridiculous things like that. She scrambled to pull down her skirt but to Gerald, she didn't seem embarrassed at all. She just regrouped and was on her feet before Gerald. She looked as though nothing had ever even happened. She had a camera guy with her, but he had this big huge camera on his shoulder and could do nothing to help her up.

Gerald scrambled to his feet just after the lady, but she had already managed to say excuse me before Gerald could, which was even more embarrassing because it was Gerald who caused all the fuss. "Ma'am, I am so sorry. I was trying to catch up to this old guy I was just talking to and ran smack into you. I'm Gerald Patterson, I am the one you are looking for anyway." He stuck out his hand to shake hers and she took it with a firm grip. Gerald thought it was a little to firm for girl, but he had heard that show business was tough and no place for pansies. He couldn't imagine anything being tougher than farming in West Texas, but his wife liked to read those magazines about all the stars and would talk about how hard they worked and how many times they got rejected. Hell, she even knew all the stars' names and birthdays along with their kids.

It all seemed like such a waste of time to Gerald but for the moment he needed this woman's help. "It's quite all right, Mr. Patterson, no harm no foul is what I always say. Why don't we go back inside where I can visit with you and your wife?" Gerald had nearly forgotten his wife and was now eager to go check on her. He led the reporter to the tiny chapel where he had left his wife. The cameraman followed them through the emergency room. They entered the chapel, but Nancy was nowhere in sight. "I'm sorry, this is where I left her. She must have gone to the bathroom or out to stretch her legs. She has been in that chapel praying all morning. Anyway, this is a picture of our daughter, her name is Ariel. She is not yet five, almost though." She took the picture and gave it to the cameraman. He did something with a scanner or something. Gerald couldn't tell what, but it didn't take long, and he handed the picture back to her. "She is adorable. Now can you tell me the story? I know that it might be difficult but it's important to get it out." Gerald told her about the storm, the winds, and the subsequent tornado.

He told her what he felt like being lifted and yanked out of the storm cellar, what it felt like to lose the grip on his only child, and the feeling of helplessness when he was being blown through the air. He had no idea all of it was being recorded and was waiting on her to set up the camera or something, but she never did. He was dreading to have to tell the story all over again when she said the cameras were on now. What he didn't know was that she knew that there were people who had been diverted to Northwest, but this was a compelling story. She needed this on the air; this was the kind of story that no matter how it ended, she would win an award and the Dallas stations would have to offer her a job. This storm was such a big deal that maybe even New York would see it. She knew she didn't belong in this God- forsaken cowboy country. She was way better than this.

She took out a business card that she knew only had the number to the main station on it. No way she was giving out her personal cell to anyone, but it was important for her to gain the trust for her story and make them feel like she was on their side. "Mr. Patterson, I am so sorry to hear that story, I am glad that you are ok, and I am certain that we can get this story out in less than an hour. Once we get it out, I will get back to you and let you know what we have found out. We will have your daughter's picture on every TV screen in West Texas in about 45 minutes. I just need time to set up outside and introduce the story. Call that number on the card if you hear anything." She jumped up from the bench in the chapel like she was sitting on a spring and out the door she flew.

Her mind was racing; she had the story of a lifetime. Movies were made of less drama than this. She had the man on camera and he could not have been more effective and genuine. Now all she had to do was set up the introduction. "Get the tripod, I want this steady as a rock. Make sure the hospital sign is in the backdrop. Oh, look! Get those dark clouds in the shot!" She was so pumped. She wanted this done and out now. She already knew the words and how it was going to be golden, how she was going to look fabulous on screen. This was it! The cameraman eagerly set up the tripod and got it in position for the perfect backdrop. Once he was sure it was right... "Got it, Judith, we are ready in three, two, rolling!"

While he was saying three, two, Judith checked her lipstick and hair one last time and tossed the mirror on the ground where it shattered. "Good evening, West Texas, we need your help in locating this beautiful little girl." The viewers would see a still- shot that the cameraman had scanned into the system while she spoke with Gerald in the chapel. "This beautiful child who loved mermaids and Barbie dolls was violently ripped from her father's arm by the tornado that left a path of devastation in our fair city. Now up to this point there have been no reported fatalities, but I fear that time is running out for Ariel, so we need your help; listen to her father recount the harrowing details of the story." The viewers would see Gerald's interview in the chapel. "It breaks my heart to have had to hear her father recount those details, he is visibly shaken and is pleading for help in locating his little girl. This Is Judith McKinney at Northwest Hospital for Channel 4 news." She stood still to give the video a clean break and the cameraman gave her the cut sign.

The cameraman was smiling ear-to-ear when he stepped out from behind the tripod. "You were golden, Judith! Flawless as ever! This is the one!" She was so pumped she gave the cameraman a high five and looked around as though she needed more applause. Of course, no one was there, and no one cared other than her and her cameraman. "Get that to the truck. Edit quickly, make sure you clean up this little spot on my forehead. It's a damn zit that I can't seem to pop. We are going places today, baby!" The cameraman was tearing the equipment down when he asked, "Are you going back in to tell him there are other injured folks at the VA now?" She was picking up the busted mirror along with her purse. "Hell no, I can't until this airs, it kind of makes the story moot if we find out she might be at the VA. Wouldn't be any point in running the story."

The cameraman stopped what he was doing. "Come on, Judith, seriously? If that was your kid wouldn't you want to know there was a chance she might be at a different hospital? It just seems kinda sleazy." Judith now stopped; she had her back to the cameraman but spun around to face him. "When the hell did you become the morality police, shit for brains, huh? You do what I say and point the damn camera where I tell you and you might get somewhere in life but if you ruin this I swear I will make sure you never hoist a camera anywhere in any town for the rest of your pathetic life. Got it?" The cameraman stood staring at her with a contemptuous look on his face. He didn't acknowledge her threat, nor would he ever. He had dealt with so many prima donnas in his career that he knew how to handle them.

The one thing he hadn't torn down yet was the camera and the one thing he hadn't turned off yet was the camera. It was still happily rolling and had recorded her every arrogant self-centered word. He would trump her if she ever tried to blame him for anything stupid...he had been employed at Channel 4 for twenty years, he wasn't stupid. He pulled the camera off the tripod but let it run in case she wasn't through. When he was certain she was through throwing her tantrum, he walked to the truck. He edited the film as instructed and even managed to magically pop the zit from her forehead. He even managed to make his own copy of her little rant.

Chapter 53

MARK WAS STILL VISIBLY UPSET over what he felt was senseless violence. He had no stomach for it. He understood that this virus they were trying to corral could be empirically destructible but there was a better and more humane way of getting it together. Annemarie could tell he was almost at the point of no return. "We have orders, Mark, and regardless of whether we have or have no orders I would still do the same. You don't know these people like I do, they are ruthless. Make no mistake, the men we just exterminated are not patriots, they are not noble, and they would have sold that shit to the highest bidder, and if we didn't stop them now, they would return with even more men and even more greed." She paused to stare at him, but he was having no intimidation tactics from her or anyone. "Bullshit, Annemarie – you killed the colonel because you didn't like him. I MIGHT be able to understand that because he was a dickhead, but you killed the mad scientist for what? He had already pissed his pants, he was no killer, he just made a bad choice. I've made a shitload of bad choices but thank God nobody put a bullet in my head for it. I shot a man! I didn't kill him, but I would have if I had been a better shot! Jesus, this is fucked up!"

Annemarie walked passed him towards the exit. Since it was just her and Mark in the room, she made a point of brushing up against him. "I can see that you are upset and confused but understand this: because of me and Wally, that bug is on its way back to Atlanta and not on a shipping container in L.A. waiting to make its way into Iraq or Pakistan. You better understand that if that happens, those idiots will use it; if not on us, they will use it on their own people and they will constantly threaten us with the use of it. This is no college game, Mr. Chief of Staff, and if you ever want to find out what it's like to wake up and mount a 4-star General, you better get your shit together, pronto." He shook his head in frustration. After what he had seen so far, he wasn't sure he ever wanted to get into her pants. Hell, she might shoot him in the head if he didn't perform well. "Now get your ass on the plane. We are headed to West Texas. We don't get to return to DC until we have the rest of that shit." He felt bad that he was walking away from all these dead people.

Their families would never know what happened to them. They would all wonder for the rest of their lives why they didn't try to contact them. They would forever regret not having said they loved them, or had forgiven an argument, or any other unfinished business. And worse, it was a secret he would have to keep the rest of his life. He hated secrets. After what seemed like an hour of walking through all the doors they had entered, they made it outside the building. Waiting for them was a Gulfstream G650.

The big ass plane that they arrived in had obviously left for Atlanta with Olivia and its deadly cargo on board. Mark could not believe the taxpayers were paying for such a luxurious plane for just three people to fly in. "Nothing but the best for a 4-star General with a thirst for blood, huh?" Annemarie let the smart- ass remark go and climbed the stairs to the plane. Mark followed but he was still pissed. Normally he would sneak a long look at her ass, but he could not and would not get over the killing that just took place. It was senseless, and he couldn't get it out of his mind. Seeing a man die was something he never wanted to see and today he had done it multiple times. Mark looked around the expensive plane and all its luxury and realized there was no one on board but the pilots and now he and Annemarie. "Where's Wally?" Annemarie was coming back from the direction of the cockpit. "Wally is securing the base. He won't be joining us. We are to get the bug and secure it." Just then the phone on her side rang. "Copy – good work. ETA is less than one hour."

Annemarie hung up the phone. "Recon had located the last vials of the bug and have it secured. We will land, procure, and secure. They found the bike in a pond of all places. Wasn't visible to the eye, ground sonar picked it up along with some fancy satellite technology. Coordination between the two pinpointed the location within 50 yards. The yellow suits just had to figure a way to go in unnoticed, very hard to do when the country is nothing but brown. Yellow stands out like a sore thumb. They heloed those guys in and they yanked it out of that pond in minutes. Best team on the planet. They are meeting us at an unused airstrip in Dumas, they think the airstrip was used by drug runners out of Mexico. This plane can land on a dime, but it will be bumpy and quick." Mark heard the engines rev up and the plane positioned itself correctly on the runway.

In seconds they were off the ground. He looked out the window and saw the massive explosion on the base they had just left. "Holy shit, what the hell?!" Annemarie gave him that cold stare again. "Couldn't risk any accidental contamination. That base is now scorched and sealed. If there was any accidental trace of that bug left behind, it's secured now." Mark was still trying to watch the explosions, but the plane was climbing and banking in such a way that he couldn't watch it anymore. "This is insane" he mumbled.

<h1 style="text-align:center">*Chapter 54*</h1>

"SO, WHERE IS SHE?" Jake was fumbling with his hospital gown. It was open in the back and he was trying to position it so it wasn't so revealing. Michelle was trying to help him get positioned back in bed. "Who are you talking about?" Jake got himself positioned just right; truth be known he was very weak, but he would never tell anyone that. "The little girl I brought in with me. She was really struggling to breathe. Me and Paul did all we could to keep her breathing. She was just so little. Hell, I didn't know what to do with a little girl and neither did Paul. I was just glad we got that bike started and made it here in time. So, where is she? Is she ok?" Dr. Washburn stepped out of the room to check on the girls across the hall.

The big man's comments reminded him that he needed to check on the little girl and the lady with the burns. Michelle stood over Jake and touched his forehead. She gave him the most loving and caring look that Jake had ever seen. "Mr. Johansson, you came in alone. You were brought in by ambulance and there was no one with you." Jake was confused. He knew he had ridden a motorcycle, a Panhead with two passengers in tow. But then he couldn't remember actually getting to the hospital. He felt sick to his stomach, maybe he had crashed. Oh my God, maybe he had crashed and killed the others. Michelle could tell he was getting upset and moved her hand to his chest. "Jake, calm down. You came in alone. You were not on a motorcycle. The ambulance report says that you were inside your crushed truck when they pulled you out. There was no motorcycle." Even though her touch made him feel better, he could not believe what he was hearing. "Doc, I came in with a little girl, cute as hell and talks a thousand miles an hour; it was me, the little girl, and a biker guy. He has a tattoo of an angel on his arm, a naked angel. His name is Paul and the little girl's name is, uh, Ariel." Michelle had not heard the nickname that had been given to the little girl, but she felt a chill come over her as she had seen the tattoo he described. "Jake, you came in alone. That we all know is a fact, but I have seen the tattoo you just described." She paused for a second and tried to process this situation. "The man across the room with the swollen face has that very tattoo." Jake tried to sit up, but Michelle pushed him back down which was not an easy task. "Listen, you've been in a serious accident, you are lucky to be alive. In fact, you've died twice, my friend. The man with the tattoo came in an hour before you. There is no way you were together." Jake laid his head back on his pillow. He was certain he brought two people in with him. Dr. Washburn stuck his head in the door. "Dr. Hundlee, can I see you across the hall, please?" Michelle looked at the nurse. "Make sure he doesn't move, I will be right back." She patted Jake on the leg and made her way to the room across the hall.

She entered the room and saw the little girl curled up in the same bed with the burned woman. It had to be painful for the lady with the burns, but she didn't seem to mind. The little girl was wide-awake and so was the burn lady. "Does that hurt? Let me move her back to her own bed." Renee furiously shook her head. "No, she climbed up here an hour ago, she is scared and needed to feel another person. She's told me about her ordeal and more importantly she has told me that my future husband has protected her and got her to where she is now." Michelle rubbed the little girl's back and looked at Dr. Washburn. "Honey, you've been in a coma for a while. This little princess came in all by herself, she was found by the side of the road. The Good Sam that found her gave her CPR and stayed with her until the ambulance came. The paramedics had to revive her twice on the way here. She is a tough little girl, but she definitely didn't come in with your husband." Renee shook her head again. She softly stroked the little girl's hair. She stared up at the ceiling as tears filled her eyes. She described him right down to his angel tattoo. "I know it was him." Michelle was trying to process what she was hearing from the room across the hall and now this one.

Dr. Washburn was also struggling to figure out how these two rooms were connected but couldn't get it done. Michelle put her hand on Renee; it was all she could think to do. "How do you feel, honey, are you in any pain?" She could see the tears in Renee's eyes. "No, I am fine. I don't feel any pain. I just want to lay here with this little angel. She is scared. Does anyone know where her parents are, at least where Jake is?" Michelle took a step back from the bed. "How do you know about Jake?" There was a silence in the room that was broken by Jake himself. "She doesn't know me but that is the little girl I brought in." Jake pointed at the little girl who heard Jake's voice and immediately looked up. She made the motion for Jake to come pick her up, which he quickly did. "I told you guys I brought this girl in, Paul and I brought her in. Someone needs to stop bullshitting me because I just figured out that the guy with the swollen face in the bed next to me is Paul. I just saw his tattoo. If we didn't come in together then how the hell did we all end up here?" Jake adjusted the little girl in his arms. Even though she was little, his chest was sore, and his arms hurt. Holding her only made his pain worse but he wouldn't dare put her down. Renee began to struggle to get out of bed. Dr. Washburn came to her side to try and restrain her, but she was having none of it. She was hell-bent on seeing if her future husband was indeed across the hall. "I need you to lay back down, please. You are going to pull out your IV tubes. Please relax and lay back down." Dr. Washburn was doing his best to control her, but his efforts were futile. "Doc, has anyone identified the man you quacks refer to as the man with the swollen face? You will need to identify him, correct? Well if that is Paul over there then I am the one person that can identify every scar, tattoo, and blemish on his body so get the hell out of my way. You can hold the fluid bag if it makes you feel better." Everyone in the room knew she was not going to be stopped so they went from resistance mode to assistance mode.

She slowly made her way across the hall. Dr. Hundlee had one arm and the nurse had the other. They had temporarily removed the IV tube so she could freely move around. No one said anything but they all wanted to see if this could actually be true. The odds of her and her husband, or future husband, landing at the VA nearly in the same room were simply astronomical. Renee made it to the room where Paul was laying. He was still hooked up to every monitor possible. So many whisping and beeping sounds, but she could tell by the arms and the sleeve tattoos that this was Paul. She burst into tears as she bent down to kiss his badly swollen forehead. "Oh my God, look at my poor baby. He is hurt so bad. His face is so swollen, my God, baby, what happened to you?" She was trying not to be so emotional, but she couldn't help it. She looked up at the doctor. "His name is Paul Boaz. He is 53 and he is AB Negative blood type. I am not sure if that helps and maybe you already know that. I am just letting you know that this man is Paul Boaz." She returned her stare to Paul and continued to softly rub his chest and parts of his swollen face. "I'm AB Negative too so if you need any blood, I'm right here." The room stirred a little when Jake announced his blood type. "That's very kind of you but that won't be necessary, I am AB Negative also. If he needs blood he is going to get it from his future wife. That way I can hold it over his head the rest of his life." It was a good tension breaker and the room got a little bit of laughter out of it. "Doctors, the little girl is AB Negative also. We had to test it when she arrived. It appears that everyone is AB Negative, at least these four folks are." The nurse had a confused look on her face as she was reading through each of the charts.

She had collected all four patients' charts so that she could possibly figure out how they knew each other. There was no connection other than the tornado, except that they had all gone into cardiac arrest and all of them had technically died. "I think all of you need to return to your beds so you can recover and we can get you back home." Dr. Washburn was trying to be authoritative, but it wasn't working. Renee made it clear that she was not going to leave Paul's side, so they brought her bed into the room with Jake and Paul. It was a little tight to have three beds but that was the best thing for everyone. Once Renee's bed was securely in place next to Paul, the little girl ended up back in the same bed with Renee. It was clear that she was not going back to being alone. "Has anyone found her parents?"

Chapter 55

GERALD WENT BACK TO THE CHAPEL where he had left Nancy to go find the reporter. She had not returned. He checked with everyone at the front desk and they had not seen her. He began to roam the halls looking for her. He even checked every bathroom. He would knock on the door and if no one answered he would just walk in and check. He even went into maintenance closets. He became frustrated and decided to go back to the main lobby. He took the same seat in the lobby where he had sat next to the old man.

The news was still covering the damage from the tornado. He actually saw pictures of his own property being shown from the helicopter camera. The governor was supposed to tour the area this afternoon, blah blah, blah. Gerald could not care less about the governor or any of that horseshit. He wanted to find his little girl and now he wanted to find his wife. Where the hell did she go? She wasn't speaking to him and he understood why. She blamed him, and he couldn't blame her for it. He had gone over the entire event in his head about a billion times now. It was like glass cutting through his skull. He did admit to himself that the conversation with the old man helped a bunch. He felt a calm he hadn't felt since the storm took his baby. He was half in and half out of his thoughts and reality when he heard her name loud and clear, right on the screen in front of him; the report of his lost little girl was airing now!

He hollered at the attendant behind the counter to turn the TV up which they gladly did. The entire emergency room got quiet either out of respect for this man's wishes or the curiosity for the report, but either way, the room was silent. He saw himself on TV, he had no idea she was recording that. He felt uncomfortable watching himself on TV. He got choked up when they showed Ariel's picture on the screen, my God he loved that little girl. When she signed off and the news anchors went back to other news, he sat back down. He felt like he had done all he could do for now. He heard a voice from someone sitting in the emergency room. "Somebody should tell that little girl reporter that they took a bunch of people over to the VA. Maybe they should check there." Another voice that Gerald obviously didn't know replied, "She does know, saw her do the report from Northwest this morning right after the tornado struck, damn reporters today are just lazy." Gerald was stunned. Why didn't she tell him? That makes no sense at all.

He knew he had to get to the VA quickly and he had to tell Nancy! Where the hell was she? We need to go now! He ran up to the front desk again, took out a picture of his wife and handed it to the attendant. "I have to go to the VA now. My wife is somewhere in here, but I can't wait to find her. When she shows up please tell her that I went to the VA." The attendant gave him the thumbs up sign and he bolted through the sliding doors. The code blue was being paged as he was exiting the building. He was on I-25 in a flash. His mind was racing – he felt bad about leaving his wife, but this was it and he knew it. She had to be at the VA. Where the hell was Nancy? He was so frustrated that she didn't stay with him; they should both be on the way to the VA.

He had no idea she had stolen a syringe from an examining room and injected air into her veins. Her heart stopped a few seconds after the needle plunger pressed its way into her system. She was gone. The tornado had claimed its one and only fatality.

He didn't bother parking; he pulled right into the emergency area, jumped out, and left the keys in the truck. He didn't care. They could have it. The entrance to the VA was a bit smaller than Northwest and it seemed more crowded. He looked quickly for the check-in counter and found what he was looking for. It was towards the back and he started weaving his way back to it. He was almost to the counter when he saw him. There was the old guy he had talked to at Northwest. The old guy saw Gerald at the same time. "Hello, young fella. I told you she would turn up." Gerald stopped and was about to ask him what he was talking about because he had no idea if Ariel was here or not. Maybe the old guy checked when he came over.

An empty gurney came between them and he looked down to catch his balance; when he looked back up the old guy was gone. Screw it, he thought, just get to the desk and they will let me know. He got to the desk and was out of breath. He took one more look back to see if he could see the old guy, but he couldn't. "Can I help you?" He spun around to the desk. "I'm looking for my daughter." He pulled the picture of Ariel from his pocket and handed it to her. "Oh, she is so cute. Hang on, we had a bunch of kids come through here but most of them have gone. Let me check." She clicked away on her computer for a few minutes. A visitor interrupted her, and Gerald decided he wanted to punch the woman that interrupted her, but decided he had more control than that.

She handled it beautifully and returned to the screen. "We have a little Jane Doe in Poly Trauma. Jane Doe is when we don't know who they are but everyone in trauma has dubbed her Ariel because of her mermaid undies. She is adorable, but she's had a rough time of it." Gerald could hardly stand in this spot any longer. There could be no mistake. He knew they sold that underwear all over the world, and the odds of another little girl wearing mermaid undies were pretty good, but he just knew that she was here. "Where is Poly Trauma, ma'am?" He was moving in a direction when he asked. He wasn't even sure if he was going in the right direction, but he felt like he needed to be moving. "It's on the 3rd floor, the elevator is just around the corner. Follow the signs. Good luck!" He was practically running when he slid into the open elevator. 3 was already lit as someone else was already going there. The door would not close. It would almost close and then pop back open. This happened a few times so he and the orderly that was headed to 3 stepped off.

There was another elevator, but it was already several floors above them. "Jesus, where are the stairs?" Gerald was frustrated to a boiling point. "Follow me." The orderly led the way to stairwell doors. "We had a busy morning. It was as crazy as I have ever seen here. I actually saved a guy's life today, well almost. I was going to if the doctor didn't get there. I did stuff today I have never done before. Are you here to see someone?" Gerald was not in the mood for small talk, especially not when he was climbing stairs. "I'm here to see if my little girl was brought here." The orderly stopped climbing. "Señor, is she about 5 years old?" Gerald nearly ran into the back of him when he stopped. "Yes, she is! Have you seen her?" The orderly smiled. "See, I saved her life too. I was just going to see how she was doing. This is good, you just need to follow me!" With that said the orderly took off running up the stairs. Gerald obliged him and stayed right on his heels. They hit the door to open into the hall of the 3rd floor and were at the nurses' station. A couple nurses scolded them for making so much noise but neither the orderly nor Gerald paid any attention.

The orderly went straight to Ariel's room. The two men burst through the door, which caused Renee to jump. Ariel was still on lying on her chest. Ariel raised her head and saw her father and she nearly jumped out of the bed she shared with Renee. "Daddy! I knew you'd find me! Daddy!" She was in his arms in seconds. Gerald had never in his life felt relief like that. His mind went back to when the tornado took her from him and now she was back in the exact same spot. He cried like he had never cried before. Through his tears, he apologized to her for letting her go. He could feel her little arms tighten around his neck and he knew she was safe. He would never lose her again. "I knew you would find me, daddy. I knew you would find me before the bad things came to get us. I kept them from getting us. They are bad, daddy. That man helped me, but they wanted him bad. We wouldn't let him go." Gerald was confused about all of it, so he went with it anyway.

Through his sniffles he managed to ask, "What bad people, baby, who is that man and who is we? Who else was with you?" Renee was tearing up as she witnessed the reunion. She was so happy to see the little girl find peace. She started to interrupt but the old man in the Navy cap interrupted her. "They are the collectors. I've been battling them nearly my whole life. They are the bad version of the white light people see when they are about go to heaven, only they aren't going to heaven. The collectors want the folks that need a change in life but don't know it. It's sort of a wake-up call if you will, scary little buggers for sure." The room was silent. The information was not handled as well as it should have been, but it was clear that the old man knew what they had gone through.

He turned to walk out but stopped and turned back to look at Gerald. "Don't worry, young man, she will be taken care of. She is safe and peaceful now." He smiled, pulled his cap off his head, brushed his hair back, and returned the cap to his head and he left. "Who was that?" Renee turned because she knew that was Paul's voice. He was awake! Jake walked into the room at the same time that Paul made his presence known. Jake looked goofy in his gown and he was so big. "You must be Ariel's pop. I am Jake. She is one tough girl, you should be proud of her." Renee was so excited that Paul was awake, she wanted nothing more than to touch him and hold him, but she restained herself. His face was still swollen, and she wasn't sure what other injuries he had. She didn't dare risk hurting him any more than he already was. She continued to fawn over Paul and started crying again. Through her tears she managed to interrupt Jake as he was speaking. "Since you are already up, can you ask that old guy to come back in here? I have more questions for him." Jake looked confused. "What old guy? I've been standing at the nurses' station just outside the door, there hasn't been anyone come in the room but these two guys." He pointed at the orderly and Gerald. Gerald turned toward the door and walked outside with Ariel in his arms. She had a firm grip on her daddy and she wasn't about to let go. Gerald asked the nurses' station if they had seen anyone that fit the description of the old guy, but everyone behind the counter confirmed with him that they had not. Paul was still very weak, and his face was still pretty swollen, so it was hard to talk but he did anyway. "Some weird shit happening here that needs answers." Gerald came back into the room shaking his head. "They said there wasn't anyone like that around. I know I saw and talked to him in the lobby of the other hospital, I was surprised to see him here." Paul lifted his hand like he was asking for permission to speak but he forged ahead without permission. "We saw him on the road here. After we made our way out of all those pastures, he was just standing on the side of the road. I thought it was weird for an old guy to be out in that location but whatever, man." His voice was so low and labored that everyone had to lean in to hear him.

Renee placed her hand squarely on his chest and urged him to rest, to not overdo it. You could see him smile at her through the swollen face. Jake stood there in his gown for a second but couldn't resist speaking. "Guys, I was out in the hall, my cop instincts got the best of me, so I got them to give me access to all our charts. I apologize if I broke any HIPPA laws, but I had to put some things together. All of us came in separately. In fact, all of us came here in completely different ambulances and I am not talking about ambulance drivers; I am talking about completely different ambulance companies. We've never even seen each other before." Moans went through the room as he said that. "I know, it makes me dizzy, but the only thing we all have in common is that we all went into cardiac arrest and technically speaking, we all died within a few minutes of each other." He paused and looked around as if he was trying to keep a secret. "I think we just saw God and the Grimm Reaper." Ariel lifted her head from her daddy's shoulders and looked around. "Daddy, where's mommy?"

Chapter 56

MARK COULD NOT SEEM TO GATHER the words. He was in no mood for discussion or explanations. He had put aside his lust or love for Annemarie for now and was trying to make sense of what they were doing. He recounted the shootings over and over in his head and could not get the image of a man's brains being blown out right in front of him out of his mind. It was nothing like Hollywood portrayed it. Each time he saw the life go out of the two men in the image, he felt sick to his stomach. He wiped his face with his sleeve and realized that his hand smelled of gunpowder, which made him feel even more nauseated.

Jesus, he had actually tried to kill a man today. He was the frickin' Chief of Staff for the President of the United States of America and he actually tried to kill a man today! This was absolute nonsense. "If you try to rationalize what we are doing, you won't be able to. How a deadly virus that nobody has ever even heard of got out of our control and was nearly in the hands of global terrorists is not something that is easily rationalized. But if you kick yourself in the gut over the lives lost today and the brutality of which they were lost, you will never sleep again. This is the ugly part of the job that the President knew you needed to see. This is why America is the land of the free and the home of the brave; this is why millions of people every year try to sneak into our country, they want to be free. In their hearts they know that there is a price for freedom and they are willing to pay it. Their price is risking it all to cross the border and our price is seeing how ruthless people can be when that freedom is threatened. I'm sorry you don't see me as the woman you used to ogle but I have a job to do and I do it well. I am a patriot and deep down so are you. We don't cower to terrorists and their fear tactics. We meet violence with extreme aggression. I am a small part of the reason why millions of Americans sleep easy. They don't know the ugliness that exists, often at their very doorsteps. Sulk and reason all you want, Mark, but you saved countless lives today and when we pick up that second batch of evil that awaits us on the ground in West Texas, you will have saved countless more. It's no more complicated than that."

Annemarie certainly had a way with words, but it didn't make him feel good. "Wally is a killer. He dropped those guys with no remorse and he enjoyed it. I can't get those images out of my head. You two had your code about playing an instrument already worked out so you knew you were going to murder him before we even went in there. It's sick is what it is." Mark put his hands on his knees and looked out the window. He could see the landscape was ugly, so he knew they were close to where they needed to be. Nobody ever went to West Texas for its natural beauty. He didn't expect a reply. "Wally is a soldier and a damn good one. He is more patriotic than you and I put together and it is unfortunate that the world will never know just how dedicated he was." Mark looked at her with a confused look. "Was? Where did his plane take him when we left? Does he get some sort of witness protection treatment?" There was sarcasm in his voice. Annemarie didn't answer him because the phone beside her head buzzed. "Copy that." She hung up the phone and buckled herself in tightly. "You might want to buckle up. This runway is short and probably not in the best condition. It could be a very tough landing." The landing was not nearly as bad as Mark expected. The plane came to a stop and there they were, eight guys in hazmat suits surrounding what Mark thought was the equivalent of a small safe.

Annemarie stepped off the plane and Mark followed. The conversation was brief, and the men loaded the safe into the cargo hull of the plane. Annemarie said something to the guy that seemed to be in charge and she motioned for Mark to get back on the plane. He quietly wondered if anyone else would get shot in the head while he waited.

Maybe Annemarie was sending him back on the plane so she could spare him another vision of yellow brain matter getting spattered all over the place. He sat there in his nice comfortable taxpayer-funded jet and thought that the people of America should know this stuff goes on. They should know that there are bad people in the world and there are people paid by the government to deal with them. If they only knew. Annemarie climbed back on the plane, grabbed the phone, and let the pilots know that all was secure. "Do the pilots know what the cargo is?" Mark still had sarcasm in his voice. He could not believe he was so infatuated with a woman who kills so easily. He thought that type of personality would be deadly, what if he didn't perform well in the sack? Would she put a bullet in his head or his privates?

The plane took off as smoothly as it could, considering most of the runway seemed to be dirt and gravel. In no time they had climbed to nearly 60,000 feet. Just as the plane was leveling off and Mark was getting a grip on things, the phone beside Mark's head lit up and buzzed. Mark glanced at it and then looked at Annemarie. "You gonna answer that?" Annemarie was stoic but relaxed in her response. "It isn't for me, it's for you." Mark smirked but he could tell she wasn't kidding. He picked up the phone and there was no doubting the voice on the other end of the line. "You doing all right, partner?" Mark could be staggering drunk and he would know Jim Stafford's voice and it actually caught him off guard.

He was not expecting to talk to the President. He wouldn't mind talking to his best friend, but he really didn't want to speak to the President of the United States, and how the hell did Annemarie know he would call? "No, I am not all right, but I am sure I will get it together soon enough. How are you, Mr. President?" Mark was lousy at small talk, even with his closest friend. He remembered sometimes they could sit in a room with each other and not say a word but be happy as clams. That's what he loved about his friendship with Jim, they didn't need to talk to reinforce anything, and they just enjoyed knowing the other was in the room. "You've definitely seen some serious stuff today, bud, you delivered like you always do. You have never let me down and you sure didn't today." Mark knew this was going somewhere but he wasn't sure. "I didn't do much. Annemarie and her guys did all the dirty work, or should I say heavy lifting." Mark knew to be discreet and not divulge any details about the day's activity on a phone line.

This was probably the most secure line in the world, but the President always had enemies. "Listen, Mark, I know you are upset about what you saw today. Sometimes the work of the people is ugly. America owes you more than you will ever know and unfortunately America will never know that they owe you. I wanted to thank you personally. As long as I am alive you will never have to worry about a thing. You know that, right?" Annemarie continued staring at Mark throughout this conversation. "I know that, Jim. Is there something I should know? You seem like you have something on your mind. As soon as we drop this bottle of death off in Atlanta I can meet you in DC. How's that sound?" There was a very awkward pause. "Sounds fine, my friend, you be safe." The phone went dead. Jim was never one for long goodbyes. Mark jammed the phone back in its cradle. "I'm going to meet him at the White House after we drop off this bottle of death in Atlanta. What time do you think we will get back to DC?" Annemarie didn't answer, she just stared at him. It made him uncomfortable. "Never mind, you are obviously preoccupied. I will ask the pilots myself." He unbuckled his seat belt and was about to get up. "There aren't any pilots, Mark." He turned to look at her and laughed. "We are flying through drone technology. We won't make it to DC. We are headed South, in about two hours we will be over the Sea of Cortez." Mark felt a knot in his stomach. The puzzle was finally coming together, and he did not like the picture it revealed.

He sat back down in the chair. "Why the hell are we headed to Mexico? You are going to want to start talking really quick, Annemarie. I have had about all this James Bond shit I can stand for one day." Annemarie crossed her legs and placed her hands on her knees. "It wasn't supposed to be this way. You have to believe me on that, this was certainly not the plan. The vial that was fished out of the pond was cracked, the team wasn't exposed but there was no transporting this beast without risking the health of the entire Southwest. They managed to house it safely in that container but because it is so new, they aren't sure how much it could wiggle out of its protective housing. They believe that it is leaking at the moment, which is why we climbed to 60 thousand feet, they figure that's a safe contained altitude. It would freeze if it leaked. They figure when we hit terminal velocity over the Sea of Cortez, we will impact the seawaters at almost Mach II. We will disintegrate on impact, so will the bug, and the world is safe again." Mark's head was spinning and without any control he began to tear up.

He was more shocked than pissed. "Why the hell did we even pick it up? Why the hell can't we parachute out of this fucking plane? It's a drone you said, it can fly on its own all the way into the Gulf. This is fucking stupid! Answer me! We have to get off this plane!" Annemarie let out a deep breath. "The minute you and I stepped off the plane to pick up that second vial we were contaminated. We lost communications with the ground and they couldn't warn us. Even though they had the suits on they were certain they were compromised. We may be on one of the most advanced planes on Earth, but it is not immune to glitches. I know it seems like amateur hour at the Pentagon but there is no other way. The President signed off on my plan before we took off. I called him from the cockpit to let him know you and I were both walking chemical weapons with a very short shelf life. The doctors estimate that we will probably be comatose before the plane hits the water. We won't feel a thing. I'm sorry, Mark." Mark tried rationalizing what was happening, but he couldn't. He said a prayer to himself and sat back in his seat. He had nothing left in the tank.

Chapter 57

THE EACH WERE RELEASED in different stages, with Paul being the last. He had broken vertebrae that needed several surgeries and recovery. He would never ride a motorcycle again, but after seeing the collector, he was good with it. He and Renee married. They took up Gerald's offer to buy two acres of his farmland and built a home close to him. Ariel was the flower girl at Paul and Renee's wedding. She was adorable as usual and was a big hit with the band. As it turned out, she could do an amazing Shania Twain imitation. Jake was the best man, which seemed strange to Renee since the two guys had not met each other before the tornado, but when the two were together it was as if they had been best friends their entire lives. Renee liked Jake very much, as did everyone, but she couldn't get over the fact that her sometimes drug running boyfriend was now best friends with a Ranger and a really poor farmer.

Jake arranged to have Nancy's funeral procession led by his motorcycle. He didn't know Nancy but somehow, he felt like he did. Her ceremony was sad and emotional for everyone but Ariel in her own way, helped every person that attended. She was special in a way that Paul couldn't describe but he found himself paying attention to her every move. In his mind she seemed to bring everyone together in a way that he couldn't fully describe and besides that, she managed to clean up everyone's language. They had gatherings quite regularly on the farm. After the tornado, something must have happened to the soil because Gerald's crops came in better than they ever had. He rotated them regularly so that he had money coming in at almost all points of the year. He never remarried; Nancy was his one and only love. It was unfortunate that he had to battle Nancy's father for custody of his own daughter after she died, but he managed through it. No way would he ever allow anyone or anything to take her from his arms.

Renee helped him with the court costs and because of her history, she knew a few bare-knuckle style lawyers that would not let Gerald get pushed around. She also helped Gerald sue the TV station for Judith McKinney's lack of honesty and won a considerable amount. The cameraman's private video of her rant was pretty much all he needed to seal the deal. Judith McKinney moved to somewhere in Oklahoma and tried to revive her career.

Mark and Annemarie were hailed on TV by the President of the United States as true patriots that were in route to a conference, and unfortunately their plane lost cabin pressure causing the pilots and the passengers to lose consciousness. Their plane flew until it crashed into the Sea of Cortez. There were no survivors and because of the depth of the water they were unable to recover the wreckage. The President actually choked up at the funeral as he was delivering the eulogy for both. He focused on the deeds and service of both, he lauded Annemarie for being one of the toughest people he ever encountered and for the loyalty and dedication that both Mark and Annemarie exhibited for their jobs and their love for their country. He spoke candidly about his lifelong friendship with Mark and made a point of saying that he would not be standing here today as President of the United States if it were not for Mark. He wiped the tears away from his face as he paused and said, "there will always be a giant void in my heart that will never be filled.

Olivia was killed in a single car crash one day after she returned her portion of the virus back to CDC in Atlanta. Her funeral was much smaller with much less pomp and circumstance. Her family attendance was small and her little brother delivered the Eulogy. He was a handsome young man that during his comments had to stop and steady himself. His voice broke up often and he fought back the tears as he spoke of her timid personality, her love of chemistry and how much he would miss Christmas without her. He concluded by saying that he was grateful for the time that he had with her and would never understand or come to grips with her loss or the circumstances by which she was taken from them. He said that she would never drive fast and that she would definitely never drive late at night so something just didn't seem right but he vowed to crowd and to his parents that he would find the truth. The police could only tell them that she was killed in a single car crash and that the car was nearly incinerated at the crash site, but there were no witnesses. The most puzzling thing was that the charred wreckage of her car had been sent to impound lot after the crash and according to the impound manager, they had somehow accidentally compacted it into a square block and it had already been shipped out for recycling. He could not find an invoice for the receipt of the car and he also couldn't find an invoice for the recycle shipment. "Darndist thing he'd ever seen."